The Autobiography
Of
Sherlock Holmes

Books by Don Libey

A Few Thoughts Before I Go

Avon Lake

Church of the Redeemable Yoohoo

Wound Down Days

Spare

Islands

Religion and Gods

God: Hit or Myth

On Gold

Libey On Customers

*Libey On Change:
Marketing Trends and Supercycles*

Libey on Recency, Frequency and Monetary Value

Libey and Pickering On RFM

Libey and Pickering on RFM and Beyond

The Autobiography
Of
Sherlock Holmes

By

Sherlock Holmes

Edited By

Don Libey, S.H.S.L.

Campbell & Lewis Publishers

San Francisco and London

Designed using fonts entirely of Baskerville Old Face
Printed in the United States of America

First Edition

ISBN-13: 978-1477479155
ISBN-10: 1477479155

Acknowledgement

Great appreciation is extended to Professor Donald Pollock, University at Buffalo (SUNY), the eminent anthropologist, Sherlockian scholar and author, who graciously read the manuscript and offered valued guidance and encouragement to the editor.

Grateful acknowledgment to Conan Doyle Estate Ltd. for permission to use the Sherlock Holmes characters created by Sir Arthur Conan Doyle.

Campbell & Lewis Publishers

San Francisco and London

For Andrea

and with memories of my parents,
Weir and Mildred Libey,
who began it all in 1952
with an eight year-old's
all-time favorite Christmas gift:
The Complete Sherlock Holmes

Preface

The circumstances surrounding this remarkable
and heretofore unknown autobiography by Sherlock
Holmes require careful explanation.

I am an antiquarian: a dealer in rare books and,
more specifically, those of four nineteenth century British authors, being Charles Dickens, Thomas Hardy,
Kenneth Grahame and, especially, Sir Arthur Conan
Doyle. I live in Sonoma County, California, at Bodega
Bay, the enchanting seaside hamlet made famous by
Alfred Hitchcock's film *The Birds*. My books are sold
almost entirely online at my modest website www.libey-
books.com. Also, they are found on the largest online
antiquarian network in the world: www.abebooks.com.
Mine is a small business and attracts little notice, being
favored by a few, random collectors and lovers of rare
first editions. We bibliophiles exist mostly for enjoying
our books, and setting up in business as an antiquarian dealer is simply a justification for purchasing more
books.

My education was in English Literature and ancient Japanese and Chinese poetry. A small volume of
my collected poetry over thirty-five years was published
in 2010, a second collection in 2012, and my first two
books of fiction were also published in 2011. Another
twelve or so of my books have been published on business topics.

Since childhood, my reading interests have included the four authors mentioned. At age eight, I received *The Complete Sherlock Holmes* for Christmas and spent the next fortnight devouring the book. This year will mark my sixtieth reading of the sacred canon.

My memberships include The International English Honor Society, The Dickens Fellowship, the Thomas Hardy Society, the Kenneth Grahame Society, and the Sherlock Holmes Society of London. I am essentially unknown in all of these prestigious literary societies, but study the scholarship in quiet anonymity with great appreciation for the intellectual insights of others. My particular interests are the first editions and variants of *The Hound of the Baskervilles.*

Prior to my antiquarian life, I was an international marketing advisor to the chief executives and boards of directors of numerous U.S. and British corporations and for a number of years lived half-time in England, residing in the Cotswolds and in London. I retired from business in 2010.

Over the more than thirty-five years spent visiting the U.K., I explored all of the great rare bookshops looking for treasures. I met a number of book scouts who unearth valuable first editions for collectors and ship them to their clients all over the world. These individuals attend the book auctions, book fairs, and exhibitions in England, Scotland and Wales, find unrecognized first editions of Dickens and other authors potentially valued at hundreds or thousands of dollars, quietly buy them for maybe the equivalent of fifty or a hundred dollars or so, and re-sell them to their eager customers for one or two hundred dollars. The book scouts are a valuable source of first editions for the antiquarian market and their identities are both coveted and carefully guarded.

One of my sharp-eyed book scouts—I will call him "Ian"—is an expert at finding Arthur Conan Doyle material. He has brought me such books as a first-edition of *The Adventures of Sherlock Holmes* in fine condition that he found in the bottom of a box in a used book stall in Bourton-on-Water and bought for five quid, offered to me for twenty pounds (for which I paid him one hundred pounds), and which I subsequently re-sold to a collector for one thousand dollars, the nominal value being at least fifty percent above that modest retail price. That's how it works in the old book business. You take care of your scouts and they take care of you.

One year, it may have been 2008, after a long three-month stay in England in my role as the non-executive director of a large British multi-unit corporation, I returned to the U.S. where awaiting me was a slightly scruffy box of books from Ian. As I remember, there was a first edition of Grahame's *Pagan Days*, several firsts of Doyle's Professor Challenger books, three firsts by Dickens, and an assortment of ephemera and other oddments he had picked up somewhere. One of the spindrift pieces was an old holograph manuscript covered by a stained and soiled blue paper wrapper with the title *Montague Notations* written in ink across the front. I put it on a shelf of a bookcase for future research and forgot it for nearly a year.

In 2009, I had a heart-attack and, during the recuperative months following, spent time cataloging and organizing my books. Re-discovering *Montague Notations*,

I sat down to explore what this curious blue-wrapper manuscript might contain.

What follows is what I discovered. After reading and re-reading the manuscript, I spent a month reflecting on what to do next. I realized that the manuscript was either a great hoax or one of the most singular literary events of all time. An autobiography of Sherlock Holmes, if authentic, would be equivalent to finding the actual autobiography of Christ, a fictional character given eternal life by devoted but delusional followers. In either case, the believers would be proven true and the nonbelievers proven false. It is a weighty responsibility.

My decision after a month was to quietly ask several eminent Sherlockian scholars for their guidance. By agreement, they shall remain unidentified, but it makes little difference as they were unanimous in their conclusions. After reviewing sample pages, and being provided the provenance of the discovery by Ian, their counsel was straightforward: publish the manuscript as is, including Holmes's penciled publishing directions, and allow the world's Holmesians and Sherlockians to decide.

So be it.

Don Libey
Bodega Bay, California
May 28, 2012

Montague Notations

Montague Notations

By

Sherlock Holmes

[perhaps give to Watson's publisher]

To John H. Watson and Mycroft Holmes:
Brothers in Loyalty, Spirit and Intellect.

Introduction

My old friend and chronicler, John H. Watson, in setting down so many of the adventures we shared over the years, had the remarkable ability to conduct the written flow of events to create sensational interest in the many cases, but only a limited ability to focus the pure light of accuracy on the essential deductive facts.

Since Watson's death this year, it falls to me to relate some of his masquerades and lapses—intentional and unintentional—made in writing up the various cases over the past nearly fifty-five years of our association and to expand upon my case history.

Having reviewed his published and unpublished accounts from his original notes and manuscripts, preserved in an old tin dispatch box willed to me by Watson and conveyed to me by his lawyers after his funeral, I concluded that a mere *erratum* of our entwined lives and careers would be massively incomplete and, therefore, have set down a true and accurate summary of our experiences within the broader discussion of my unique life and career; in effect, an autobiography.

While many of those who grasp the elegance of pure reason and deduction prefer to keep Watson's writings *in situ*, others share my obsession for accuracy and intellectual purity. The clearest path to that elegance is to leave the published works of Watson unchanged, but to shine the brilliant illumination of the comparative beacon upon them for all who prefer to possess absolutes rather than the shadows of vagaries.

The cases as described by Watson embody his interpretations constrained by his good and honest emotions, whereas at the center of the work lies my developed intellect and rarified reason within the cold clarity of scientific detachment. The result, after all else has been discarded, is truth. And, as this pure truth was produced by me and brought to bear on so many important events over so many years by my tenacity against the evils of crime, it is my responsibility to those individuals in Great Britain, Europe and the United States who have, in recent years, begun to show interest in the science of criminal detection through their study and analyses of Watson's writings to provide an accurate factual foundation upon which to limit emotion while resolving problems and combatting the ever-expanding evils of mankind.

To these ends, I have devoted myself this past year. Now, at age seventy-seven, long since retired to my rooms in Montague Street, time has decreased my energies and output, but my routine of five hours of writing a day over sixty-two consecutive days has produced this account of my life and career providing those who have interest with the full and accurate history of the world's first consulting private detective.

Sherlock Holmes
London, 2 July 1929

I came into the world as Sherlock Holmes on Tuesday, 27 January 1852 at half-four in the afternoon— tea time. My mother, Virginie Verénet Holmes, bore me in her canopied bed at our ancestral home, Church Court, in Maiden Wood, Isle of Thanet, Kent, where she had born, in order, my older brothers Mycroft and Wittrell and our sister Juliette. I was last in birthing order. My father, Parkford St. John Holmes was absent.

My earliest memory is of my brother Mycroft placing different lengths of string on the floor of the nursery when I was one-year old. Two years later he explained to me that it was an exercise in learning to judge the lengths of things without needing a measure. To this day, I can determine the length of an object from across a room to within a half-inch.

Wittrell, who became a mathematician with the Bank of England upon his graduation from Peterhouse, Cambridge, taught me to manipulate numbers relative to space and organization when I was four. Like him, my ability to deduce the exact speed of a train by counting the number of telegraph poles passed in a one-minute period of time was a simple calculation of distance and time to arrive at the precise, accurate speed of the train. Wittrell would later serve in the highest ranks of government as an unimpeachable auditor of Crown assets.

Similarly, Mycroft developed his mind to 'see' answers to questions that were impenetrable to others, and rose to be not only unimpeachable, but also indispensable to the monarchy, the government, and its ministers; indeed, he *was* the government. His wide network of upper-class contacts was forged during his years at Trinity College, Cambridge where he took his Master's in Classics.

Juliette was taught by Mycroft and Wittrell at age six to observe the changes that occur to metals when the acid to alkaline balance shifts. In her early twenties, after taking her Upper First in chemistry at St. Andrew's, she became the sole and final arbiter of authenticity for the precious metals bourses of Great Britain, Belgium, The Netherlands and France. During the Great War, Juliette alone was trusted by the governments of the Allies to maintain the authenticity of gold and silver bullion flowing between Britain and Europe to finance the war against Germany.

The Holmes children were born in 1840, 1844, 1848, and 1852. At my birth, our mother was thirty-nine years old and our father was forty-two. Mother died in 1895. Father died in 1891. Mycroft died in 1926. Wittrell died in 1928. Juliette died in 1924. None of my siblings married or had children. I am the relict of the family. All of us resided in London, that great machine of human excess, depravity, creativity and—rarely—beauty.

Parkford St. John Holmes was a successful international factor. He financed various enterprises and, owing to a Holmes family trait of making accurate deductions through logic and reason, experienced virtually no financial losses over his career. As a prominent

Anglo-European factor, he became a wealthy man and, signifying more, he retained and grew his wealth.

Father was imposing. Tall at over six feet and muscular at seventeen stone, he created a powerful impression; yet, he was soft-spoken and reserved. His eyes were an unusual light-hued gray-blue that gazed through anything he looked at, whether a person, an object, or a distant landscape, making him seem detached and almost other-worldly. Mycroft alone inherited his eyes and his formidable size, as well as his detached and reserved nature. In both, however, the outer veneer of detachment masked the roaring minds working within their large cranial vaults. Father could calculate the cost, weight, and profit of a ship's hold full of coal to the penny instantaneously without setting pen to paper; whereas Mycroft could calculate the entire catalogue of diplomatic chess moves between two political opponents or two feuding nations in the same blink of those familial eyes.

Father belonged to the Diogenes Club in London where Mycroft would succeed him in later years. When he was in the City on business, he used the club's visitors' room for occasional firm matters, but was most often found at his accustomed place at the Exchange where he was regarded for his high integrity, his firm negotiations and his flawless financial transactions. His definition of integrity extended equally to his personal life. He neither smoked nor drank, the only exception being a glass of Burgundy or Bordeaux wine during Mother's formal dinners at Church Court.

At home in Maiden Wood, Father was supportive of his tenant farmers and often extended to them sums of money to better their holdings and increase their production. While recorded in the ledgers as loans, many were either forgotten or payments were never requested. No farmer, however, ever received Father's favours if he was a drunkard, a lay-about, or mistreated his wife or children.

Virginie Verénet Holmes was Belgian, the daughter of Walloon aristocracy. Schooled in Brussels and Paris, she was, in later years, a philanthropist using her inherited family wealth, gained from European private banking, to benefit and strengthen Belgium's equality for women and to further the early suffrage movements of Europe. An intelligent, capable and strong woman, she continued to successfully manage the family business for four years after our father died, selling it for a princely sum to a large French factoring firm only a month before her own death.

Mother was above mid-height, slim and possessed her superb figure throughout her life. Her shoulder-length hair was dark, thick and rich, of shades of mahogany and oak, lustrous from many brushstrokes each morning and night. Her features were elegant, with a thin, sculptured nose perfectly placed among aristocratic facial bones and dark eyes of smoky, languid teak. Graceful and elegant, she moved like a swan: efficient, gliding, never disruptive and making no wake. Her voice was gentle, low-pitched and always quiet, demanding one listen attentively to hear what she said.

Juliette received the full measure of Mother's beauty and graciousness; indeed, they looked nearly twins as they straddled their respective years of early and middle womanhood. Wittrell was a blend of both Mother and Father, the only such blend of us all. I was the male version of Mother externally and the detached calculating machine of my Father internally. A number of my cases resulted in my assuring reasoned justice for the criminal, my Father's influence; a number resulted in my assuring reasoned compassion for the criminal, my Mother's influence.

Mother was an accomplished harpist, having studied under the great maestro Parish Alvars during his 1883-1884 hiatus in Paris from his position as First Harpist of the Imperial and Royal Opera of Vienna. As a child, I would stand next her gilded concert grand harp, idly plucking melancholy scraps of sound from the strings, a fascination that would follow me during my years of violin-accompanied intense concentration on criminal problems.

As children, we all had more attention from our mother than from our father, given his frequent absences due to business, as well as his reserved nature which, to a degree, extended to his children. Father was an influence, but we received affection or what was perhaps love from our mother. And, Nanny Dobney.

Nanny Dobney arrived prior to Mycroft's birth and remained with our family until her semi-retirement when I went to university. She then became nanny to a prominent Surrey family for another twenty years, a career of over forty years with only two families. She retired to Camberwell where she delighted in periodic visits from her then adult charges. Juliette was particularly good about visiting Nanny; they were very close as Juliette was the only female out of the eight children Nanny raised during her career.

Nanny Dobney had a soft, ample figure. As children, we all delighted in her welcoming lap and arms as she read us stories or listened to our questions. Her hair always smelled of violets, even when it had turned silver. She wore a gold locket and only once showed us the picture of a young soldier inside.

Nanny used logic and reason in her life lessons, whether on nature rambles or in discussions of choices and consequences. Her soft voice was never raised and she never resorted to even the mildest forms of punishment; she simply enlisted our cooperation and devotion.

Church Court is an early, eighteenth century, stone, gray pile of a country manor house on the Isle of Thanet. It is built upon the site of at least one prior house dating back to feudal times. The family holdings covered a large portion of land in Maiden Wood, as well as foreshore and docklands fronting on the English Channel. Our father's firm, then in its third and last generation of Holmes ownership, factored corn, coal, minerals, and ore between England and Europe and its fleet of cargo ships used our ancestral lands as their home port as they moved between London, Amsterdam and Calais. For many generations before the establishment of the family firm, Church Court had been the feudal *demesne* of the Holmes family which had a long history as the minor squires of Maiden Wood, involved in agriculture and deriving rents from the thirty or so tenant farms across the family lands. As the only remaining member of the Holmes family, I retain ownership of Church Court but have not lived there since my university days. The house has been rented for income since our mother's death and the farms were gradually sold to the farmers who held the tenant lifeholds.

The year after the birth of Mycroft, Mother and Father removed to a villa in the south of France near

Nice where they lived for a year. Similarly, one year after the birth of Wittrell, they decamped to Lake Como for a year. And, a year after Juliette's birth, they resided in Venice, returning after nine months due to the heat. My first birthday was observed at a villa on Lake Geneva where the now numerically larger Holmes family lived during 1853. It was there, during reportedly pleasant hours of conversation at a lakeside coffee house, that my father became acquainted with, and thereafter maintained a many-year correspondence with, a brilliant private tutor in theoretical astro-mathematics who would, in later years, have a profound influence on my career, and I on his.

As a family, we enjoyed, of course, the privileges of prosperity and class. As children, we were given the manners and social capabilities expected of families in our place in society. Our parents frequently gave parties, dinners and week-end 'stays' in the country for a diverse and interesting circle of their friends that included writers, politicians, government ministers, artists, explorers, actors and scions of business. My mother particularly enjoyed inserting strong, passionate feminists into the mix of guests to assure stimulating and lively interchanges during the long and elegant dinners at Church Court. Contrary to the family conventions of the time, our parents always included the four of us at dinner and we soon all learned not only the art of conversational repartee, but the nuances of an intellectual society.

Memory calls up one of my early fascinations with the long dinners. The table, with the six members of our family and numerous guests, was laid with the full array of Victorian-era tableware, china and crystal. From my seat near the end of the table, the flawless order and alignment of the silver and various plates and glasses the full length of the table captured my mind and my growing affinity for precision. I learned to not only memorize the original positions of all the objects on the table, but to memorize the changes to the implements and dishes made by each person during the course of the dinners. Even now, these many years later, I can recall the exact progression of a salt cellar's migrations during a celebratory birthday dinner for my mother.

In addition to Nanny Dobney, our family was well cared for by a housekeeper, a maid, a cook and a butler. The cook and butler were married—a Scots couple from Inverness, Hume and Mrs Hume. The housekeeper was a highly-efficient woman from Kinlet, Shropshire, Mrs Hodgson, whose proclivities included an intense dislike for tobacco smoke and an eternally gray outlook focused on temperance and moderation in all things. She was a counter-balance to the Humes who were both jolly Scots Pagans who celebrated life and a liberal sampling of the Tantalus and gasogene. The loyal household was brilliantly managed by Mother who maintained equilibrium and equanimity among all.

At age ten I was given a pony that I never liked. It was given to a neighbor a year later. Horses remained thereafter, for me, an essential attachment to a Hansom cab. I did, however, benefit from the close study of the imprints of horse hooves and shoes and, some years later, wrote a detailed monograph on the determination of breed and age from hoof prints and the classifications of the distinctive hammer and punch marks of county farriers.

My youth was solitary. Mycroft took the part of my childhood friend; in reality he was more like my mentor given the twelve years difference in our ages. From age six when I began my schooling to age nineteen when I left for university, my associations were almost entirely those of Nanny Dobney, my family and the family friends and retainers. The child-like innocence so valued by others never found its way to my early years; I was born middle-aged and remained there, a fixed point in unchanged time.

The Holmes squires had a long history of educational progressivism. My great-grandfather established a school for Maiden Wood in 1770 complete with a qualified headmaster and a carefully chosen staff of instructors. Over its now one-hundred fifty-nine years of service, Thanet School has not only educated the Holmes offspring but—due to my ancestors' successive liberality and vision— those of the tenants and villagers of Maiden Wood, as well as numerous progeny of the landed gentry in the near environs of Kent who were accommodated as tuition-paying day-scholars. Over the years, many of the school's sixth form graduates went up to Oxford, Cambridge or other desirable universities of the realm.

Unlike my father and brothers, as well as prior Holmes males, all of whom graduated Cambridge, I was admitted to Exeter College, Oxford where I took an undistinguished Ordinary in natural sciences. While my siblings achieved Upper Firsts and Masters Degrees, my largely self-directed studies were outside the academic tolerance of even the progressive leanings of Exonian dons. Fortunately, I competed well at fencing and was tolerated primarily for my ability to excel at foils against Exeter's sister college, Emmanuel College, Cambridge.

I went up to Oxford in October of 1871, and came down in May of 1874. Aside from a skill for fencing, I acquired a working knowledge of organic chemistry, but little else. And, again, unlike my father and siblings, I made no important contacts or friends who would have any lasting importance in my later career. I entered life self-contained and I shall leave it in the same manner. Only three people have penetrated my detachment to be regarded with what may pass for affection but which was, in fact, admiration: Mycroft, Watson and 'The Woman.'

During the years at Oxford, my time was divided between studies in chemistry at Exeter College and an informal course of eclectic studies in numerous of the other colleges of Oxford. There existed in my mind the idea that I would learn chemistry and other sciences along with abnormal history and human criminology and, by so doing, bring science to bear on criminal activity, a worthy use for a superior intellect in my estimation. And so, I took knowledge from wherever it was to be found; all colleges and all disciplines were fair game for my self-directed education. A morning would find me in the laboratory; an afternoon in the dissecting rooms; evenings in various college libraries reading the history of crime and criminals. An experiment with human blood or enzymes often led me to specialty laboratories at various colleges equipped for specialty analyses and thence to another college's library with a collection of historical treatises on mass murders, serial deaths or military executions. I viewed all of the colleges of Oxford as being my personal resource for knowledge, a concept that shattered the linear conventions of an institution nearing nine-hundred years of unchanging, insular existence.

It was in my third year at Oxford that the raw elements of deduction were linked for the first time in my brain. The physical observation of wet grass, linked with the chemical knowledge of ash, linked to a unique boot print, linked with the psychological reaction to fear, linked with the analyses of time and distance, linked with geographic certainty of a surrounding neighborhood, all came precisely together to produce a flawless, serial, analytic deduction taking me to a specific room in a specific house where a specific crime was about to take place by a specific criminal with murder aforethought about to occur; and the instantaneous linkage of all those elements into a cohesive and accurate deduction coursed through my brain like lightning, and I emerged another person, forever to be more machine than corporeal.

At that moment, my studies were complete. I possessed the essential knowledge, deductive tools and connective synapses to inhabit the center of the organ of crime and defeat its purposes. My brain was on fire and would burn with a white-hot intensity for decades to follow.

2

There is only one city in the whole of the world that can nourish white-hot intensity: London.

After coming down from Oxford and spending a week at Church Court, I departed on Sunday, 31 May 1874 on the second full moon of the month, for London. My father made over a generous allowance to me for expenses, but I accepted only a small annual stipend of one-hundred guineas from him until I could make my own way.

I chose the British Museum as the centre of my web in order to have access to its vast library and reading room for historical research. Close by also, were the great stations, Covent Garden, and a number of the hospital laboratories wherein my researches were to continue. After only three nights in a boarding house in Holborn, on 4 June I located satisfactory rooms at 47 Montague Street, Bloomsbury, next the Museum to its east, between Russell Square and Great Russell Street. The owner, an antiquarian specializing in Byzantine studies, lived quietly in rooms on the second floor and fitted the ground floor as his extensive library and museum housing his arcania. Mr Arbuthnot let the entire third and fourth floors, furnished, for a quite low rate likely owing to his complete lack of knowledge of the prevailing economics of 1874 due to his oyster-like existence lived almost exclusively in the Byzantine Era, and, having lost the previous tenant to the attractions of opal mining in Australia, had immediate availability on the day I noted his 'To Let' sign next the entry. We came to terms and I removed my few belongings to my new lodgings within the day.

Arbuthnot employed a housekeeper-cook, a maid, and a boy-in-buttons to service his and his lodger's needs and his shop requirements. Arbuthnot was unusual in that, as a young man of twenty-five, whilst serving in a book shop in Great Russell Street, a collapsing bookcase fell upon him and rendered him unconscious for a full day due to the blow, affecting the limbic area of the brain. When he awoke, he no longer possessed the sense of smell. He was, for many years, a perfect landlord for a tenant prone to noxious chemical experiments and the near-permanent acrid fog of tobacco smoke above stairs.

And here, in the interest of accuracy, I must begin to clear away Watson's persistent use of protective red herrings throughout his many narratives of our years together. Watson always feared retaliatory malice from the criminal world, especially as my reputation grew. He wrote consistently and imaginatively of our lodgings at 221B Baker Street and of our landlady-housekeeper, Mrs Hudson. Watson mentioned Montague Street as my former lodgings only once in his description of our first meeting and, subsequently, our taking rooms together at 221B. But, it was not in Baker Street that we shared rooms; it was always 47 Montague Street where I have lived continuously for over fifty-five years and where, for a number of those years, I intermittently shared rooms with Watson. There was no Mrs Hudson. The housekeeper-cook employed by Arbuthnot was Mrs Vestal Hunter to whom Watson attributed all of the gracious qualities of the long-suffering, but fictional, Mrs Hudson. Mrs Hunter, in 1874, was a most capable woman of only twenty-two years of age. Her husband had been tragically killed in a train accident, and she had a daughter, Violet, who went on to be a governess. After Arbuthnot's death in early 1896, I purchased the Montague Street property from his estate and provided Mrs Hunter with a lifehold on the portion formerly occupied by Mr Arbothnot. She remains housekeeper today, now seventy-seven years old, healthy and quite happy in her spacious ground and first floor rooms. We have provided a cook and maid who care for our respective retirement quarters and modest needs.

The second floor has a large, comfortable sitting-room facing the street and two smaller rooms at the rear, one that serves as a combination library and study and the other a bedroom with a small en suite. Two large bedrooms on the third floor face the front and the rear with a full en suite between, installed after the Great War. Paralleling the bedrooms to the north is a long lumber-room with a collection of paraphernalia, oddments, costumes, commonplace books, and other flotsam of the years. Meals can be taken in either the sitting-room or the third floor bedroom owing to the convenience of a dumb waiter also installed after the war which connects to the kitchen below stairs. During the Watson years in residence, beginning in 1881, he preferred the third floor rear bedroom overlooking the gardens while I occupied the second floor bedroom adjacent the sitting room, an arrangement that admirably suited my often nocturnal and inconsistent habits. Watson liked his sleep undisturbed. And, it must be said, he was a prodigious snorer and his third floor rear bedroom suited us both.

The only length of time when I did not lodge at 47 Montague Street was the period following on the Reichenbach Falls business when, again as a protective device against retaliation, and as a safeguard against the possible necessity for future hiatuses, Watson described my wanderings on the Continent and beyond in various disguises, but primarily as the diffuse and fictitious Sigerson. Again, accuracy requires a correction. I returned from Switzerland having spent a week hidden in various agricultural wagons crossing France, finally boarding *incognito* one of my family's coastal freighters at Saint-Nazaire. Two days later, I was safely tenanted as a bee-keeper on a small holding in Maiden Wood and passed the years 1889 to 1891 as Colin Fraser, apiast. It was during those bucolic years that I wrote *Practical Handbook of Bee Culture, with Some Observations Upon the Segregation of the Queen* which Beach & Thompson kindly waited publication until 1910 when all danger had passed.

The sitting-room was—and is—largely as described by Watson. The bullet holes remain where I idly placed them; the Persian slipper continues to give service; the old side-board is in its accustomed place; and the coal-scuttle next the fireplace still holds the cigars, pipes and accoutrements of the habitual user of tobacco. Little has changed in the interior furnishings of a life during a long passage of time when, without, all has changed. Here, in my old and familiar rooms, with the thick, yellow fog at the windows illuminated by gas-light, it is always—and always will be—1874.

3

With my nascent web established within the narrow confines of the British Museum and Montague Street, I began extending its threads into four major sectors: crime, police; high society; and commoners. Crime fuelled my enterprise and my bloodlust; the police provided the necessary, ultimate sanctions; high society provided the income; and the commoners provided the variety and perversions of victimisation that stimulated my interests. In total, my 'organisation' encompassed the four opiates of evil, good, retribution and reward. And I could pick and choose which strand of my web to tighten and which to relax in order to achieve the stimuli I desired. There were cases where I allowed the criminals to lead the chase; others when I chose the police as the scent hounds; still others where the commoners were the whippers-in; and sufficient other cases where high society was allowed to be the Masters of the Hounds for the benefit of their guineas. All of my cases had one common element: I alone in this entire system of crime, punishment, victimisation and reward possessed the precise and accurate deductive solution owing entirely to my superior intellect and singularly developed skills of observation and reasoning. Mine was the perfect career for a precision brain motivated by a rational ego and the tantalising knife-edge of good and evil. Had my father's innocent coffee-house conversations with the astro-mathematician during the months at Lake Geneva in 1852 ever grown into an influential mentoring or retainer position with our family for that supreme titan of evil, I could have just as easily supplanted him as the Napoleon of crime and established my web for wholly evil purposes, such are the hair-trigger dualities of my unique powers and singular personality. Fortunately, the bulwark that was Mycroft and the essential Watsonian goodness prevented my experimentation with the dark skills.

Watson did not join me at 47 Montague Street until 15 January 1881, on the cloudless evening of a bright full moon. Within a month, we were involved in the Jefferson Hope murder case which Watson was to call (in response to my suggestion) *A Study In Scarlet*.

There were, however, six and a half years prior to Watson's association when I lived in my Montague Street lodgings alone. During those unobserved years, from June 1874 to January 1881, I had begun to build my practice and develop my web. The last half of 1874 brought only seven insignificant cases—two burglaries, a missing one-armed chestnut roaster, a Malay sabotage of a Thames barge, an obvious murder of passion, the odd disappearance of four Hansom cabs in one evening, and the one case earning over one-hundred guineas, the return of Lord Sedley's kidnapped albino Macaw.

The following year, 1875, strengthened my relations with a number of Inspectors of Scotland Yard who became curious as to my powers of observation after I conducted an analysis of a murder scene in Seven Dials leading to the apprehension three hours later of a Punjabi oil renderer from the Norwegian whaling ship *Nordkapp*. I concluded fifteen successful cases that year and two others that were unsuccessful. Actually, both were technically successful in that I solved the crimes, but they were both petty crimes driven by family poverty and I quietly restored the stolen items to the owners and turned a blind eye to the deeds of necessity by these lesser, repentant criminals after delivering a strong warning.

My practice grew in 1876 to twenty-eight cases, half of which were requests for my assistance by five respected Scotland Yard Inspectors. Six cases were engaged by members of London society and earned enough in fees to make the year profitable. Three cases by landed gentry allowed me to increase my account at Capital and Counties Bank to the equivalent of nearly two years of expenses. And one case concerning a peer brought a small reward but a great amount of recognition in the high society quarter of my web. Among the titled of the realm, my name was frequently mentioned in drawing rooms of the great houses in reference to "The Case of the Moonlit Apple." Perhaps one day it can finally be told, as only one person intimate with the horrors of this old and respected noble family remains alive, albeit irretrievably insane.

By New Year of 1881, my casebook had one-hundred and twenty-three synopses of problems brought to me. These were the cases that pre-dated Watson's association and our first problem together, the forgery case. Most of these early adventures were simple and unimportant; a few were interesting; one or two were unique; all were essential to creating a reputation allowing me to pluck out of the miasmic effluent of British and European crime a few precious gems that reflected original evil and enormous creative energy. Only vaguely aware of an unseen presence at that time, I was, indeed, preparing for Moriarty.

4

During my first year in consultancy, I came to understand the necessity for responsive and reliable assistants to enhance my awareness of activities and persons and efficiently conduct searches throughout the teeming boroughs of London. A young boy of the streets, then about twelve years of age, often undertook errands for me as needed. He conveyed orders and parcels between me and my tobacconists, Shervington's, in High Holborn Street and could be relied upon to place my notices in the agony columns or send telegrams at any hour. Arthur Wiggins became essential to my effective functions. As he rose in rank, Wiggins became my Sergeant-Major, commanding a squad of Irregulars who regularly took the equivalent of the Queen's shilling in our private war against crime, ranging across the chaos of London, going everywhere, seeing everything, overhearing everyone. The Irregulars were each paid a shilling a day plus expenses with a guinea bonus for the boy who ran to ground the object of the search.

Wiggins went on to a successful military career; indeed, rising to Colour-Sergeant during the Great War where he served with distinction in France. He retired from the Blues and Royals and, as one might expect, entered upon a long third career of service as a Commissionaire in his old haunts in Holborn. From time to time, I continue to rely upon his good and trustworthy character for my most important needs. Even

Mrs Hunter has come to welcome Wiggins's visits, and he her sumptuous afternoon teas.

Another lasting association of my formative early years in practice included that of Mr Morris Angel, the Shaftesbury Avenue bespoke costumier from whom I learned the intricacies of disguise and theatrical make-up. Mr Angel and his son Daniel supplied the costumes and related goods to many of the London theatres and music halls, having begun over thirty years previous with a small clothing rental service in Seven Dials. Over the many years of our association, Mr Angel conveyed the techniques for changing my appearance quickly and effectively, including the manner in which height and age could be altered and, as needed, even gender. The Angels were generous, giving me access to their numerous storerooms in the scattered theatre districts where I was able to fix up small 'bolt-holes' into which I could disappear and reappear as a totally different person or go into hiding for a day in order to avoid detection. I also kept an assortment of old clothes and a box of make-up, facial appliances, crepe hair and spirit gum in the lumber-room of my lodgings, and within a few minutes, could leave from the entrance of number 47 as a ship's carpenter, a green-grocer, an antiquarian, a country vicar, or an ostler as required.

An odd acquaintance—indeed, more than just that—was Sherman, the taxidermist in Pinchin Lane, Lambeth. From time to time, he loaned his brown and white, half spaniel, half lurcher scent-hound, Toby, to me to trace one of my fleeing quarry. In his youth, Sherman had been game-keeper for Maiden Wood and had often accompanied my father in tramps throughout the holding and on many a day's shooting with guests. He had retired to his bird-stuffing business at Lambeth prior to my going up to university, and I often passed a quiet hour and a pint with him whenever I was near Pinchin Lane. A naturalist by self-training and one acutely aware of the behaviour of mammals, Sherman could be relied upon for shrewd insights into the likely movements of criminals gone to ground. I sought his knowledge on numerous occasions, even more than the service of his incomparable tracking-hound, Toby, particularly for information on the physical and chemical changes in dead tissues exposed to the weather. Sherman died in 1903. It was only due to Mycroft and me settling his affairs after his death that we discovered that he had held the Royal Warrant from the Prince of Wales for taxidermy of royal grouse and pheasant; such was the high regard for his talents. Apparently, many of the birds displayed at Balmoral are Sherman's work. He also made a good living between 1896 and his death providing scores of displays of preserved red grouse perched on small wood logs to Matthew Gloag, the Perthshire whisky maker who gave the birds to publicans selling his Famous Grouse whisky. I miss him and his connection to the Maiden Wood years and our family.

My banker for thirty-four years, from 1874 to 1910, when he retired, was the taciturn Scot, Mr Ian Tarquin Campbell, of Capital and Counties Bank, 125 Oxford Street, London. Mr Campbell was of great service on various occasions when it was necessary to provide extreme and confidential security within the bank's vaults for certain priceless royal jewels, government documents, sensitive foreign treaties, and other items central to my cases. He also was custodian of my personal monetary holdings, most of which was converted to gold due to my preference for the portability of bullion should it be necessary.

After Mr Campbell's departure, my affairs were taken over by Mr Alistair Threadway in 1910 who continues as my personal banker at Capital and Counties to the present, eleven years now since its merger with Lloyds. These two men managed my financial affairs with scrupulous integrity over a period of now fifty-five years and relieved me of having to intrude valuable brain capacity with the everyday concerns of money. During a period of nearly six years, I even entrusted the management of Watson's finances (at his request) to Campbell after the good doctor found himself too often a plunger on a limited income. All of my bills are sent to and paid by the bank, and every fortnight a packet containing twenty pounds is dispatched to me via messenger for my cash needs. Any unscheduled expenses that may arise are paid by me using cheques I carry in my bill case. This routine has been followed for nearly fifty years, except during the hiatus when it was managed by Mycroft.

A few others are or were long-time, trusted acquaintances over the years. Bruno Schiava, the Neapolitan chef at Simpson's has been a valued fixture at twice-weekly dinners for many years. Samuel Cundey of Henry Poole & Co was my tailor when I came to London and Poole continues to make my clothes today. Mr Cundey took over the business from Henry Poole who had dressed my father for many years. Mycroft and Wittrell were also life-long customers of Mr Cundey and Poole & Co and visited their premises at 15 Savile Row twice a year. Like all Holmes males, they were buried wearing bespoke Poole. I distinctly remember Cundey's admonishment to a rag-tag young man fresh from university, intent upon making a name for himself in mid-nineteenth century London: 'Dress well, Mr Holmes, and the rest will take care of itself.'

Writing of our family tradition of wearing Poole to the grave, I should like to recount here another Holmes family tradition, one that may seem quite bizarre, but which, I can assure, has great, practical antecedents. The minor squires of Maiden Wood, going back to feudal times, many generations before my father and grandfathers, have followed an ancient Celtic tradition of burial in unmarked, unknown graves. As the relict, I will be the last to be buried in this traditional way. When a Holmes dies, he or she is conveyed to a woodland burial ground known only to the family and laid in a linear line from east to west in rows ranked by the century. There are no monuments or markings of any kind, only gentle mounds of thick, lush, greenwood moss among the ancient oaks. Only our memory remains for those who will live but briefly beyond our own years. When we are gone, it is as if we never existed.

5

Watson and I were much the same age. He was born 25 February 1852, less than a month after I was

born. Over the years we spent together, on occasion—
often after several glasses of port and the intimacy of a
warm fire on a winter's evening—Watson would recount
aspects of his life which gave one a more fully-furnished
understanding of this most solitary man.

John Henry Watson was born in Cirencester,
Gloucester to Henry and Martha Watson. Henry was
Sexton of Church of St John the Baptist, a medieval
church dating from 1115. He was christened John for
the church and Henry for his father. He styled his name
John H. Watson throughout his life.

Henry Watson began service to the church as an
Acolyte, rising to Verger after ten years. He was entrusted with the duties of Sexton, a particularly responsible
position given the age of the works. After thirty years of
service, his name was effaced from the church records
for reasons unknown, but apparently due an unfortunate
occurrence owing to a debilitating weakness for drink.
He died alone, a broken man no longer in control of his
mind or his life.

Martha was an embroiderer of church vestments,
having talent with both the needle and elegant design.
Her work was in demand for many years until her sight
diminished to the point of near-blindness in her later
years. She died several years before Henry.

Watson's elder brother, four years older, was
Christened Henry John Watson, also named after his
father and the church. He read canon law and became a
clerk to the doctors of the ecclesiastical courts of the An-
glican Communion where he concentrated on probate
cases involving the church and inheritance. He inherited
his father's failing with drink and died equally unhappy.

Watson alone was destined to achieve a measure of success and happiness. After significant hardships due to his chronic lack of money, Watson took his degree of Doctor of Medicine from the University of London in 1878. He was a staff surgeon at St Bartholomew's Hospital, but had little in the way of lucrative work and, given the attraction of subsistence and excitement went out to Afghanistan, the graveyard of empires, in 1879 after a brief period of Army Medical Department training at Netley.

During the battle of Maiwand, 27 July 1880, whilst attached to the 66th (Berkshire) Regiment of Foot, upon transiting a dry river bed, Watson sustained simultaneous wounds to his shoulder and leg fired from Jezail muskets by a sniper party of Afghans in ambush within a depression in the elevated river bank. He was sent to the rear to a field hospital where his wounds were cared for and then to England where he was convalesced through the autumn of 1881. He was given a medical retirement due to his injuries and debilitation along with a small wound pension insufficient for independent living and lasting only nine months. Soon after, on 15 January 1881, Watson and I would be acquainted and would begin on a long association together.

Watson's constancy with me in our adventures together belied his essential peripatetic nature. It is not a disservice to say that, while competent as a doctor, medicine was not Watson's passion; indeed, it can be said that his later literary endeavours, the extensive body of published works retailing the cases that came our way, was a passion greater than his chosen profession. Watson, to my certain knowledge, never achieved significant financial success as a doctor. He set up or purchased three practices and earned a fair living, but he was not of the cut to become a Harley Street name and earn a large income. His practice in Paddington began in mid-1888 and he was back in residence in Montague Street in late 1889. The second practice was located in Kensington beginning in late 1890 and continued until he sold it in mid-1893. During these years, he continued to share rooms with me, as the small practice consisted of an examining room and waiting room only with no lodgings above. His final practice was in Queen Anne Street from 1902 through 1905. Again, he continued in residence in Montague Street during these years. The only years when Watson maintained his residence elsewhere during our long association of forty-eight years, from 1881 until his death this year, were the fourteen months in 1888-1889 when he resided in Paddington and the three years following on the Moriarty business when I was *in absentia*.

It is not entirely accurate to say that Watson and I shared the same rooms all those years. When he began his final practice in 1902, we had the third floor converted to private rooms for Watson. The larger bedroom became a sitting-room and he moved his sleeping and dressing room to the smaller bedroom. Over the course of the years 1905-1929, Watson and I lived together, but apart, much as lodgers in separate rooms in the same house. There were months—indeed, years—when we did not see each other, only hearing the other come and go on our vastly different timetables. Even during Watson's return to the Army Medical Department from 1913 through 1918, he remained in his rooms, as his duties were those of Senior Medical Officer at the London Recruitment Centre that processed young men joining the army and the navy to fight in the Great War.

Watson married in 1888, just a month before he began his Paddington practice. His wife was, in his words, 'An intoxicating, wild Welsh girl with a voice like a golden harp.' Her name was Tegan Astley, from Llanwddyn, Montgomeryshire. She was a cytologist who prepared and interpreted microscopic tissue specimens at St Bartholomew's Hospital. Watson had made her acquaintance when he was a resident surgeon in 1879 and they walked out together for several years after his military service prior to their becoming engaged in 1886 and, subsequently, wedded on Saturday, 18 June 1888, on an auspicious, symbolic full moon that was to be of short duration. Watson asked me to be his Best Man and, of course, I agreed. The wedding supper was at Simpson's and the next day Watson and his bride left for a week in Wales. Upon their return, he set up his practice in Paddington in a modest house with the examining rooms on the ground floor and their lodgings on the first and second floors. Ms Watson assisted with the patients in his surgery and Watson was happy and content.

Watson's happiness would end eleven months later with the death of Ms Watson and their baby son during childbirth. He was never quite the same afterward and, in desolation, returned to the comforting familiarity of our rooms for the rest of his life.

Watson's deep sorrow manifested itself, as one would expect, through his writing. When he set down the final version of *The Sign of Four*, he veiled within his narrative a romance and subsequent marriage to Mary Morstan, another of Watson's fictions that was meant for every good reason; in this case, for his own emotional preservation. He was paying homage to the great love of his life, Tegan, now lost; creating, as it were, a wispy period of happiness as a balm for his sorrow at the loss of his family. Watson was never married to Mary Morstan, or any woman other than his beloved Tegan. For Watson, she was The Woman.

Watson possessed valour, loyalty, integrity, and tenacity in great measure. No matter the turns our adventures together took, I could rely on Watson absolutely and without fail. I sometimes regret, especially since his death, that I never gave him proper credit for his steadfastness. Watson would positively beam at the smallest compliment, and I never paid him enough of those human utterings that mean so much to so many.

As Watson was also the relict of his family, I took care of his final arrangements following his graceful death from old age and, both breaking with and upholding the traditions of an ancient and honourable people, laid him among the mosses, next to my future resting place, in the peaceful Maiden Wood grove.

6

In his writing, Watson touched lightly on Stanley Hopkins, the young and promising Scotland Yard detective whom I assisted to solve the murders of Sir Eustace Brackenstall, Peter Carey, and Willoughby Smith, among others.

Hopkins, who was thirteen years my junior, was born at Maiden Wood where his family had been farmers for generations. My great grandfather had made over a large farm to Hopkins's great grandfather in gratitude for saving the life of his son, Parkford, who was to be my grandfather. Parkford had been working in a large harvest barn storing corn for the winter when the building caught fire from an oil lamp explosion. Hopkins's great grandfather fought his way through the inferno, climbed up into the high loft and threw Parkford down onto the thick sheaves of corn below. Then, jumping down himself, he slung Parkford over his shoulder and made his way through the flames to an opening in the lower portion of the doomed barn leading to four box stalls where horses had been stabled. They both escaped alive just as the flaming barn collapsed onto itself; another few minutes and they both would have been killed.

Hopkins attended Thanet School, excelled and was sent up to University College, London where he studied geography and geology for two years before leaving to seek employment when his family could no longer afford to maintain him at university. Knowing I was in London, his family contacted me requesting an introduction to people of my acquaintance who might have a position for young Hopkins. A discreet inquiry and a good reference led to an interview and he was soon offered employment within the administrative staff of Scotland Yard. Within two years, he was given an opportunity to transfer to investigations and his career as a detective was begun. Ultimately advancing to the rank of Chief Superintendent, he retired in 1917 and lives at Kew.

Hopkins was a favourite of mine during his years at Scotland Yard. Among the many official detectives I have known in my long career, the best of whom were mediocre, Hopkins was the exception. He alone came close to understanding something about my methods and applied himself to learning from me through observation. He requested my assistance in twenty-three cases from 1887 to 1888 and from 1891 to 1910. Hopkins gained positive notice from his superiors early in his career, during 1888, when he was one of many detectives working on a disturbing series of murders. He brought me a great deal of information and I consulted with him as to possible threads that would lead to the killer. By using my methods and following my lead, Hopkins explicated numerous obscure points about the killings in Whitechapel that impressed his superiors and led to his future rapid advancement to the rank of Inspector and beyond. While the killer was not apprehended due to the reluctance of several ranking Chief Inspectors to allow me to investigate over fear of the possible public exposure of Scotland Yard's inability to deal with the situation, the superior investigation of elements of the killings by Hopkins resulted in internal support for scientific methods that would, one day, lift Scotland Yard out of the anti-intellectual slough of despond inhabited by the likes of Inspectors Gregory, Gregson, Jones, and—to only a slightly lesser degree—Lestrade. While not inherently bad men, the bog-standard Inspectors all possessed willing but plodding minds incapable of advanced reasoning, deduction, synthesis, and accurate conclusions. To his credit, Hopkins never allowed his ego to dominate his reasoning capacity, a valuable trait that, I believe, I assisted him in appreciating.

To their credit, those in the highest ranks at Scotland Yard did immediately request my assistance in 1900 just prior to the queen's visit to Ireland. The Boer War had caused a great deal of unrest and the government had uncovered evidence of an assignation plot against the queen to take place during her visit. The success or failure of the plot revolved entirely on a series of encrypted messages giving the details and timings of the movements of the assassins. The knowledge of the messages flowed immediately to the Prime Minister through Mycroft and, within hours, I was given full access to the coded communications. As the queen neared the coast of Ireland, I successfully isolated the book from which the messages were coded, using an encryption device Watson and I had encountered in an earlier case. The book's specific page number, line, and words are enumerated and the message assembled from the various words so selected. The difficulty is in finding the exact book and edition that both the sender and the recipient would have access to and that would provide the identical content to be referenced in the messages. Once I reasoned the identity of the book, I was able to interpret the messages and the assassination was prevented. The book was a newly published and obscure work titled *The Great Boer War* by a British author named Doyle. A copy was found in a London library with pencil markings associated with the messages, and the writer of the coded messages had conveniently provided his name when requesting the book at the library. Even Scotland Yard was able to effortlessly apprehend the would-be assassins following my deductive work. Sometime later, Mycroft advised me of a forthcoming knighthood, but it was forgotten in the turmoil ending a great era upon the death of the queen. In any case, I should have respectfully declined the honour, the successful solving of the problem through the application of a superior brain being sufficient reward.

During the many years I assisted Scotland Yard, there were numerous instances of my having advanced the Yard's acuity in the forensic sciences. After Faulds and Galton introduced the potential of fingerprints, I began studies of methods of classification for use in comparing prints recovered during crime investigations. Advising both Haque and Bose, who had partially developed the Henry System of fingerprint classification out in India, I was able to make sixty-three specific improvements in both identification and sub-classification that led to the adoption of their basic system in 1901 by the Metropolitan Police. These improvements were detailed in a monograph I wrote on the subject titled *Improvements on the Henry Fingerprint Classification System with Emphases on Whorls, Loops and Arches and the Importance of Accurate Dactyloscopy.*

Scotland Yard also quietly accepted my research into the deterioration of dead tissues over time. Using amputated limbs requisitioned from hospitals, I placed tissue samples in dozens of glass laboratory plates and exposed half of them to the elements on the roof of a hospital and the other half in a windowless storage room on the same roof. All of the samples were examined every three days for a one-year period and notations made as to the process of necrosis, colour, weight, consistency, infestation of maggots, and other changes associated with the putrefaction of skin and muscle tissue. Across the dozens of samples, a measured scale of necrosis was developed that allowed me to accurately determine the age of dead tissue to within two days and whether the tissue had decayed indoors or out of doors. To my certain knowledge, seven murderers received the final justice in the first two years alone following my forensic advances in this important byway of investigation.

Another body of research was shared with Scotland Yard and became a singular reference source for most of the police throughout Europe. Titled *Toxic Plants and their Efficacy in Murder*, the reference work contained descriptions of over three hundred poisonous plants and plant parts and their individual toxicities, symptomologies, laboratory identification, and systemic effects along with a compendium of known instances of their use in murders. Nearly thirty-five years after its publication, it remains the last word in the criminology of biological poisons.

My relations with Scotland Yard have been symbiotic over the years and across the varied capabilities of those in charge. The Inspectors and their ilk, as well as the senior command officers have been both helpful and obstructive. They welcome my inevitable successful outcomes, but disdain my methods, although the public credit for solving the crimes is invariably theirs. I am left with the balm of knowing none of them are my equal and all of them can but only admit the verity of that fact.

❧

7

There was one extraordinary case that came to me on Thursday 1 June 1882. The case was never written about and never received any notice, but it has its own *outré* elements and should be recounted for its uniqueness in my experience. I will attempt to relate it as the good Watson might have done.

* * *

We had just completed a late breakfast and were making our way through our various newspapers when Mrs Hunter announced a caller at half ten. The look on her face indicated extreme disapproval, often an auspicious harbinger of an interesting case.

The caller mounted the stairs one at a time, the sounds of which clearly indicated a deficiency of the right leg. Upon entering the sitting room, he only partially filled the door, being less than five feet in height and of slight build. He was oddly bundled in an open great coat, with the collar raised to obscure his face, unusual for such a mild day. He leaned upon a blackthorn stick, worn at the end and scarred by gouges and gashes as if used by a beater raising pheasant from the gorse on a shoot.

"You would be Mr Holmes," said the high, wheezing voice muffled by the coat.

"I am," Holmes replied. "And this is my associate, Dr Watson. I perceive you have come from Gravesend from a berth on a five-master in the China trade."

"How you know that is beyond me, but your powers of insight attest to your reputation."

"It's merely inferential observation. The mud on your boots is that of the silt from the Thames, of a colour found only in the Bermondsey loop of the river. The cross-hatch weathering around your eyes is seen only on sea-faring men with long exposure to lengthy voyages, but the pierced Chinese coin hanging from your fob is conclusive. The head of your stick has been carved skilfully in the likeness of the Chan patriarch which is often used by first and second mates in the China trade as a superstitious talisman of good fortune and a mark of identification among the sailing brotherhood. Of course, the China trade is dominated by five-masted ships. The conclusions, therefore, are inevitable."

"Correct on all points, Mr Holmes."

"How may we assist you, Mr . . .?"

"It's Farkin. Toresh Farkin, First Mate of the *Shorin*, recently arrived from Shanghai."

Farkin turned and removed his coat. Turning back to face Holmes and me, we saw a face—indeed, a thoroughly malignant presence—as ugly as the senses can conjure. The grotesque standing before us was not only misshapen, but so horrible as to instantly create fear within the minds of those gazing upon it.

"Yes, I do that to people," said the First Mate, aware of the spreading sense of revulsion in the room. "You see in me the ravage of a diseased birth in Bengali.

Only a cruel mother would allow such a cursed product of gestation as this to live."

"The world is furnished sufficiently with the misfortunate," Holmes replied. "But you have risen far in your trade to reach First Mate of a five-master, Mr Farkin."

"Knowledge and seamanship when spliced with the unnatural fear I inspire can be a powerful source of discipline and leadership when twisted properly. I've been fortunate to serve under an understanding captain for over twenty years, beginning as sail-mender, working my way up to t'gallant-man, then to Bo'sun, Third Mate and now First Mate these last six years. It is the good captain for whom I have come to seek your help."

Holmes has an infallible sense for knowing when a case will be sufficiently *outré* to engage his interest and his energies. The sharp, piercing look in his eyes signalled his desire to know more from our freakish visitor. He reached for his cherry churchwarden and a generous pack of shag from the Persian slipper, a sign of a long and thoughtful focus on the story to be told.

"Please, lay the essential facts and details before us," he said, indicating a chair and motioning the visitor to be seated.

The First Mate filled little of the chair with his underwhelming body, but his essential ugliness seemed to fill the sitting-room, seeking escape from the light exposing it to view. His skin was yellow-gray, blanched in places, pustular in texture, made taught and shiny by scar tissue and old lesions of an undetermined aetiology. His hair was gray, what little was left. Great patches had withered and thinned, leaving him looking moth-eaten. Even his malformed ears no longer had anywhere to hide without long hair to cover them. Such physical damage could only have come from an obscure tropical disease apparently infecting his poor mother prior to his birth. The result was the most appalling physical specimen I have ever experienced in my medical career. He began to speak.

"It all began fifteen years ago while the captain was coasting the *Shorin* out in the Malays. We picked up bits of cargo anywhere we could, filling the hold with odd-lots of spices, wood, oils, textiles, anything we could buy cheap or trade for and sell at a profit in the Asian and European ports. In November of 1866, we called at Kuantan where we loaded tin and rubber bound for Singapore. We were four days in Kuantan and the captain turned over the cargo loading to the Ballast and Cargo Master and disappeared ashore. On the third night of his shore leave, an old Jakun man came aboard with a note addressed to me on a small piece of dirty rice paper on which was written in Bengali, 'Follow this man and come to me.' It was initialled by the captain, 'N. P.' The familiar initials showed me the note was indeed from Naprush Palahl, my captain.

Leaving the ship, I followed the Jakun man through the twisted and narrow alleys leading from the docks into the dark heart of Kuantan, a quarter filled with evil houses offering every possible perversion and vice within their dank and rotting cells. Ancient Malay crones pulled at my sleeves, seeking money or my desires for their opium or spirits; old men with blackened teeth leered with their promise of slave trade pleasures. Finally, upon reaching a low house with mould covering its exterior boards, signed only by a carved five-leaf lotus on the teak plank door, the Jakun motioned me to follow him into the dark interior. The floor was covered with filthy rugs, and smoke-grimed woven fabric was hung from the beams to divide the space into small compartments where sallow-faced men lay prone on hard pillows, oblivious to reality, lost to the vapours of their narcotic mixtures.

'Farkin. Here.' The voice of the captain's laboured whisper broke the dead-silence of the vile hole. Looking through the curtain, I was brought to my knees as if struck between the eyes with a belaying pin. Curled on the filthy rags covering the cell was the captain, wan and pale, and attached by its hideous mouth to the vein on the right side of the captain's neck was a giant rat, fat and bloated from its nocturnal blood feast.

'Don't' kill it, Farkin,' came the plea from the captain. 'We need each other; there can only be death if it is killed.'

'It's monstrous, captain,' I cried.

'Yes, but it is my monster and it must continue to live. Help me back to the ship, Farkin. I am so weak now, and unable to walk without help.'

I carefully detached the rat's mouth from the neck vein using a long opium pipe as a pry bar. Once detached from its unholy communion, the rat stretched itself and I could see it was at least a yard in length and its thickness had to be a foot or more in diameter. Coming as close as I dared, the stench from its horrid hair was so repulsive I had to turn my head and wretch from the wave of nausea that engulfed me there in that disgusting and degrading Kuantan hole. When I turned back to the captain, I was horrified to see the rat crawling into a leather bag that the captain then secured with a tight square knot. When I helped him to his feet and we started out from that foul pit, the captain lifted the bag holding the rat and brought it with him as we emerged into the darkness of the Kuantan night and the drear, diseased air of that accursed port.

Back aboard *Shorin*, the captain made his way down to his cabin, clinging to the bulkheads for support, dragging the leather bag with its unspeakable contents behind him. Turning to me, he whispered, 'Thank you, mate. When we are stowed and ready for sea, set sail on the first tide for Singapore. I will be here in my cabin.'

We eased out of Kuantan harbour at two bells on half-sail. As we cleared the Kuantan River Reach, I gave orders for a two-day course and we braced into the South China Sea under full sail. Pacing the deck behind the helmsman, I thought about the contamination hidden below decks and was filled with dread for the days ahead.

On making Singapore for offloading our cargo at the docks, the captain with his leather bag left the ship and I fearfully watched him disappear into the village of shanties extending a mile or more from the docklands. He was gone only a few hours and returned aboard empty-handed and sober. For the rest of the trading season, there was nothing abnormal about the captain; he was his usual quiet self. He never mentioned to me the horrid night of the giant rat or offered any explanation for the abomination I had witnessed in that Kuantan opium house. For nearly fifteen years now we have sailed together, increasing our trade and moving from coasting to the long runs of the China trade with all of the profits those cargos bring."

Holmes asked, "What has brought you to me?"

"Mr Holmes, it has begun again," replied the Bengali mate.

[Editor's Note. Here the narrative abruptly ends with the ink notation 'to be finished after April' and the initials 'S.H.']

8

Watson's obsession with protecting me manifested itself through his creation of an elaborate constructive mythology of my life. In his extensive writings, which are quite simplistic regarding my methods, but quite accurate regarding the general details of the cases, he always sought to masquerade locations, obscure dates, alter names, and re-direct the reader's attention to places and circumstances at great distances from my actual location, all designed—in his mind—to assure my safety from the latent powers of the *tentacles Moriarity*. A case in point: Watson's imaginary Great Hiatus placing me in exotic locales, wandering throughout Asia, disguised as one 'Sigerson' when, in fact, I was safely *incognito* at Maiden Wood. Watson's literary fictions rarely detract from the base facts of the cases and exist outside the historical recitations demonstrating (at least) his grasp of the broad flow of events while missing entirely the reasoned chain of deductions emanating from a unique and invincible brain.

The corpus of writing that Watson produced over the years, taken as a whole, is remarkable for this constant protective turn of the narrative. If an antagonist sought to predict my methods or whereabouts from my past actions, Watson provided only red herrings as nourishment. The extent of the protective, fictive alterations in the writings is nearly universal; indeed, were it not for the central events of the cases, I would be at a loss to know what Watson was writing about most of the time. A case set in Cornwall actually occurred in Northumberland; another described as taking place in Surrey was conducted in Lancaster; Watson's literary map was vastly different from the real locales of the cases we shared, and his efforts were entirely aimed at my protection for which I am eternally while unnecessarily grateful.

At my urging, Watson also protected nearly all of my clients to some degree. My career and its monetary rewards were founded upon the bedrock of discretion, and Watson protected that essential hallmark. Bohemian nobility may have been a mask for Spanish aristocracy; wealthy Americans may have been wealthy Italians; remote Pacific islanders may have been Hebridean clan chieftains; all was illusion; all was discretion and protection: from danger, from impropriety and from scandal. And, in sum, it was profitable to the ends of reducing criminal influences and producing a competency of fees.

Fees, while secondary to accurate deduction and intellectual stimulation, were, nonetheless, essential; indeed, I had always my living to get, and expenses were considerable. Payments from nobility are generally tokens of appreciation, often jewels or other ornaments, in the time-honoured tradition of never paying out actual cash. Monarchs believe that a small jewel graciously tendered from their hand is ample reward for great services by a commoner, a belief that is both convenient and economically effective. One Austro-Hungarian monarch of my acquaintance had snuff boxes with flawed rubies made up by the dozen for such ersatz rewards. The monarchs provided notoriety and caché; the gentry provided most of the cash.

My fees varied based on the circumstances of the client. Those without means paid nothing; those with means paid moderately, dearly or princely, depending on their station, financially and morally. I admit to a penchant for extracting large sums of money from the aristocracy and the very wealthy. Part of my pleasure in doing so derives from the fact that the wealthy are often so intimately involved with crime, duplicity, greed and the rancid spoils of habitual poor judgment. They are, indeed, fair game.

My account books, complete and accurate, albeit encrypted so only I know the actual identity of the clients, show my average income over the forty-six years from 1874 to 1920 as being over twelve-thousand pounds *per annum*. The average number of cases *per annum* was one-hundred and thirty. Therefore, the average fee per case was a bit over ninety-two pounds. In point of fact: the nobility, aristocracy and gentry paid over two-hundred pounds a case; the middle and upper classes paid about fifty pounds; and the working class paid from naught to twenty-five pounds per case.

Average annual expenses, including living expenses, were one-thousand five-hundred pounds *per annum*, thus leaving ten-thousand five-hundred pounds for either investment or interest-bearing accounts. Over the course of my career, after all expanses, I earned nearly half a million pounds which, when invested at three percent, produced nearly a million pounds *in toto*. My initial deduction has been proven correct: crime pays.

9

I never married. I was never engaged to be married. I was never what is referred to as being 'in love.' Women were simply not essential to my life. Where others preferred to devote large portions of their intellectual energies to their relationships with women, I preferred to focus entirely on my personal interest: the study of crime in all of its forms. One can fill the lumber-room of the mind with many things, or one can be highly selective as to what constitutes a worthy object for storage. My practice of cerebral retention was one of asceticism; my mental processes were greatly similar to those of a yogi: dressed only in a spare cloth, standing on one leg, the mind fixed intently on other worlds, and physically content with a few drops of water and a few grains of rice upon which to live. Time and space and appetite did not exist for the complexities of women.

Irene Adler was a woman I respected. She was a worthy opponent. I admired her mind. Other women who were central in my cases may have caused a momentary admiration for their insight, or their loyalty, or their intelligence, even their compassion; but Irene Adler possessed a multiplicity of traits to be admired and respected. However, respect and admiration was as far as I was willing to go; to even consider an emotion such as 'love' demands far too much space in the mental lumber-room to ever be profitable. Important and essential things would have to have been removed in order to have found space for such temporary and ephemeral shades as love or affection.

Evolution has predisposed the human to pursuit. Humans pursue multiple things: sustenance or caloric heat, warmth, shelter, survival, reproduction, pleasure. These pursuits tend to be visceral. But there exist the rare individuals who pursue cerebral things: creativity, power, wealth, knowledge, logic, philosophy. It is the cerebral pursuits that engender passion and artistry; that all-consuming intellectual drive that fences out all distractions which might interfere with the exquisite purity of purpose.

For me, the passion was the purity of logical deduction. I chose to apply that passion to crime, but I could have easily applied it to mathematics or science or bee-keeping. But the singular passion is not inclusive of rival passions; room exists only for one, dominant passion. And when that one passion is recognized, pursued and mastered, what evolves, given a well-equipped, disciplined brain, is genius. And when one emerges a genius in one's chosen pursuit, one has chosen to forego all other lesser passions. This conscious decision is not pathology: it is choice.

The zenith of my genius was not at Reichenbach Falls. Reduced to brute strength and luck, my ascendancy over Moriarty was, indeed, the nadir of my career. When he was gone, I had no parallel genius with whom to contend, and it had been accomplished not by genius but by physical force. That was a hollow victory and one that would be reconciled only by several years of exile and introspection. There was no triumph of genius, just the randomness of strength and balance. In his plunge to the waters below, Moriarty took with him my cerebral power, my passion, my genius. Who was the winner?

And so, I was forced to become even more rigidly disciplined to my passion if it was to survive. When I later returned to London, my apprenticeship through Moriarty over, I began the reconstruction of my genius with an increasing scientific and nationalist service preference. The discipline excluded more of what others considered 'normal' interests. I still enjoyed music, a good dinner, the occasional ramble, even the theatre now and then, but the potential distractions to a life of pure reasoning and deduction were kept at bay.

Even if I had chosen to include women in my life, I would have been a poor stick of a companion. My social skills are virtually non-existent; I have no desire to associate in society; I am essentially humourless; and I am quite unable to compromise, even to preserve harmony. The woman who would have had me would have had to have been equally as hopeless as I in prospects.

There it is. One can only conclude that I was a creation of myself, and it was only as myself that I could have existed.

10

Whilst privy to so much of my life, Watson was, during our entire association, unaware of my other passion and shadow career. Even Mycroft had no knowledge of my diversionary endeavours in the years from 1900 to 1920.

Stimulation is central to my intellect. Without stimulation I am a machine without power; my mind races, producing no worthy utility. Only stimulation creates the necessary electrical reactions required of my particular and singular genius.

My stimulants are of a variety that circle the corresponding centres of the brain. Tobacco enhances my concentration; music enables my capacity for synthesis; sitting on a pillow for hours in *za Zen* concentrates and empties my mind in order to fix upon the one inevitable truth of each case. Each stimulant involves my sensory apparatus, thus freeing my brain to work and process data at exceptional speed and insight.

Under Watson's admonishment, in 1899, I stopped the intermittent use of tropane alkaloid as a stimulant to heighten my sensorial perceptions. The replacement I chose was extreme olfactory stimulation taken to its highest level. With an intensity of study and mastery surprising even to me, I immersed myself into the art and science of perfumery. I became a 'nose,' one of the rare 'acutes' with the capacity to follow their circuitous olfactory pathways into the deep, hidden byways of the brain where, propelled by aroma alone and using the olfactory nerve access to the core brain, other universes are revealed and a epiphanic, pure form of truth and crystalline elucidation occurs. Simply stated: to discern is to know.

The fall and winter of 1899 found me often in Jermyn Street, Mayfair, at the perfumery of William Penhaligon, holder of the Royal Warrant for perfume and soaps to Queen Victoria and one of London's distinguished masters of perfumery. In the great laboratory, with its banks of rare botanical elements, essences, solutions, tinctures and distillates, I would spend up to sixteen hours a day developing my abilities to structure aromas. The workbench, known as "The Organ," was a large curved rack with ten levels that surrounded the perfumer, like a massive church organ with its banks of stops. Each level held one-hundred small glass bottles with stoppers, one-thousand botanicals and chemical formulations in varying dilutions gathered from all over the world. The Organ was the heart and soul of the perfumer's art and, like its musical namesake, it was where the perfumes were composed and performed. Even the language of perfumery uses musical terms, such as 'notes' and 'harmonies' and 'themes.'

With some modesty, I must admit to a natural ability for perfumery. Where most 'noses' require ten, twenty or more years to reach mastery, William Penhaligon himself admitted I had absorbed all he could teach me in those six months of obsessive study in 1899. With his words, "Mr Holmes, you were born to be a nose and to 'see' truth through your art," he signified my ranking with those who have mastered the perfumer's traditions.

One of my most accomplished formulas was the basis for Mr Penhaligon's final, minor adjustment in 1901 and, I am pleased to recall, was launched in 1902 as "Blenheim Bouquet," one of the firm's immortal fragrances and one that was considered as an entirely new direction in scents. During its formulation I tried over one-thousand variations while working at The Organ for over two-hundred hours to finally arrive, simultaneously, at the celebrated finished scent and the total deductive insight that led to the completion of the most difficult case in my entire career, that of the cannibal Jainists of Covent Garden, an obscene perversion of mankind that can never be revealed to the public. My solution was due to absolute perceptive clarity stemming from my use, in the final formula, of four drops of a six-percent solution of ylang-ylang for the top note. This triumph of aromatic blending triggered a further triumph of pure deduction and logic; all other debris was swept from my mind, and what remained was the truth and final solution. I had synthesized the perfumer's art and the criminologist's art and had passed into a new state of enlightenment through stimulation.

In 1901, I assembled an extensive Organ of my own and housed it in a small shop located in Great Russell Street only a few blocks from my rooms. The premises were a 'half-shop,' one divided into two from a single full-sized shop. The next-door tenant was Dorsett's, the renowned bespoke umbrella-makers to European royalty only. Initially, I used the shop as a combination bolt-hole and secluded sanctuary for concentration. In 1905, however, a former Penhaligon apprentice named Silas Wheeler who, upon qualifying his nose, had gone to work for the elegant London perfumer, Creed, came to me when Creed moved his business to Paris. He suggested that he take over my now fully-furnished and unparalleled Organ to create a line of scents under our combined names to be called Wheelock's. After consideration, we agreed to proceed under the trade name Sherler's and soon had sufficient custom to pay expenses and provide Wheeler with an ample salary. By 1910, Sherler's had become a favourite of the gentry and was honoured with a Royal Warrant from the Prince of Wales for eau de cologne. In 1920, I presented Wheeler with my Organ and full-ownership of the firm and he continues in business today, a solid and respected success.

Before Wheeler's expansion into the umbrella maker's half of the shop in 1920, Sherler's had a small front service counter and customer reception. Located behind was the laboratory and The Organ. Two smaller rooms were behind the laboratory, one was a bedroom with en suite and the other was a storage room for shop supplies. Many evenings, I worked at The Organ and often retired to the bed chamber rather than return to Montague Street. Oddly, the clarity I gained during my hours at Sherler's was extraordinary when compared to that gained in my rooms. It was, doubtless, the absence of tobacco. Tobacco smoke is the bane of perfumers and is never allowed in the laboratory or the shop. While a fog of shag concentrates my absorption of a problem, the crystalline atmosphere of the laboratory is where the discernment of truth occurs. And I must have both in order to function at the level of genius that I demand of myself. Mycroft, who has cerebral abilities that outpace even mine, has evolved his nose and palette in much the same manner, except he has done it through the mastery of obscure Highland whiskies.

11

Every case—and there were many—that I was concerned with over my long career was stimulating. I can recall all of my cases even now, and I can present the salient facts and deductions leading to their linear classification and storage. Another method of classification, however, presents far more interesting possibilities. I have, from time to time, sifted my cases into their degree of stimulation. Some were barely stimulating, others moderately so, and some were highly stimulating. But, a few were supremely—exquisitely—stimulating. One recalls these cases in much the same way as one recalls the three or four bottles of vintage Bordeaux that go beyond all other vintages and produce a sublime taste memory that endures forever.

At the summit of stimulation is the case Watson called *The Hound of the Baskervilles.* Next is *The Speckled Band.* Third is *The Musgrave Ritual.* Fourth is *The Devil's Foot.* And fifth is *The Dancing Men.* Of course, Watson had his own preferences; these, however, are mine and, in the end, it is my mind that is stimulated or not. These five cases were more than just interesting puzzles and each offered differing degrees of the narcotics Danger and Death.

Many of my cases were concerned with deduction alone; some inferential and some mathematical. Often they simply involved the finding of a notable gemstone, or a government document, or an indiscreet photograph. Deduction, to be maximally stimulating to me, is best associated with Danger and Death. The three elements become symbiotic; each sets each of the other in motion; the three in motion together cause my brain exquisite pleasure. And that pleasure is the only exquisite pleasure I allow into my sphere of experience. In the opposite dark side of the mirror, it is the same pleasure that the murderer feels at the moment life leaves his victim. Triumph. Supremacy. Power over life. Blood lust. The ultimate consuming stimulation.

The essential act, however, is to keep the mirror intact. Should the mirror ever be allowed to crack, the opposites will be forced together and—in suspension like oil and water—will fight for dominance. To be a genius in one's chosen world, one can never allow control to shatter or an internal fight for dominance to begin.

The moment one allows the mirror to crack, genius departs and brutishness ascends. That is what happened that morning on the precipice of Reichenbach Falls. So much depends upon the strength of the glass.

12

I have reflected on the potential for the perfect crime of murder during my long career. Only one case involved a perfect murder by trickery, but Culverton Smith may have come as close as anyone in my experience to creating the perfect death by the use of poison. Of all the poisons available to the murderer, bacteria are a particularly virulent and ambiguous form of poison. If the delivery of deadly bacteria to the victim's bloodstream is sufficiently ambiguous, proof of intent to murder is exceptionally difficult. As with Smith's attempt on my life, it was not even necessary for him to be present.

Potentially lethal bacteria can be had for the taking quite easily. Septic dressings and the suppurations of necrosis can be had from any hospital bin. The infection of a needle, or a thorn or a splinter of glass is straightforward and, generally, not particularly unusual. Similarly, the use of bacteria from animal husbandry, resulting in unusual but not suspicious death, such as anthrax, does not immediately suggest murder; rather, it suggests only that the victim contracted a deadly disease from an animal or a farm. If the murderer is only reasonably intelligent and minimally clever, premeditated, bacteria-induced murder can be easily mimicked. With an acute mind behind the crime, perhaps only one out of twenty investigators will consider even the slight possibility of murder.

Other lethal toxins lend themselves superbly to the perfect murder, provided they have a direct and immediate route to the blood or the nervous system of the victim. Curare paralyses the nerves of respiration, causing almost immediate suffocation; the fumes of *radix pedis diaboli* produce near-instant insanity followed by death when the concentration is sufficient; the natural toxins of the swamp adder or the *cyanea capillata*, when their bite and sting appear accidental, can effectively shield the quiet murderer from exposure; and, of course, the oft-encountered charcoal poisoning and asphyxiation due to carbon monoxide have been used with great success by legions of subtle killers.

Of the fifty-odd murderers I encountered in my career, there was only one who staged a perfect murder, and one that I recognized only after the killer was long out of reach in Brazil. Young John Hector McFarlane was duped not by Jonas Oldacre, but by Oldacre's actual murderer, Otho Cornelius, who had assumed the identity of Jonas Oldacre when I flushed him from his priest's hole at Deep Dene House in Lower Norwood. Cornelius had murdered Oldacre and, in league with his wife, established himself and her as Jonas Oldacre and the house keeper, Mrs Lexington, in order to plunder Oldacre's wealth and implicate the unsuspecting young

McFarlane. The brilliance of Cornelius lain in the fact that the circumstances of his dramatic emergence created the expectation of acceptance of his identity as Oldacre by McFarlane, the spurious housekeeper and, by extension, the police. No one questioned whether Oldacre was, in fact the real Oldacre. After killing Oldacre, Cornelius had transferred all of Oldacre's money into his bank account under his own name and, during the period immediately after the discovery when McFarlane was released from police custody and the matter was resolved, Cornelius and his wife, upon his release as Oldacre for want of evidence of conspiracy or attempted murder by Scotland Yard, quickly transferred their ill-gotten monies to Brazil and set sail for Rio de Janeiro under new names. Both the real Oldacre and his money had disappeared; his body was never found. Cornelius was never traced and the murder of Jonas Oldacre was perfected by a cunning murderer whose greatest accomplishment was in using my own ego as the instrument of his success. Lestrade's praise, ". . . this is the brightest thing you have done yet . . ." was sufficient to close my eyes momentarily to the potential of an imposter.

Watson was kind in his setting down the case of the Norwood builder, particularly as he was privy to my failure to pursue the thread to its end. In some ways, I believe, it was a *quid-pro-quo* for one or two of his own eclipses which are not found in the stories and that best remain in shadow.

One confessed murderer—Leon Sterndale—benefited from my mother's compassionate bent which, from time to time, has kept me from acting upon all that I have deduced. It can be argued that the perfect murder is, perhaps, accomplished far more often than thought as a result of the selected non-intervention by a compassionate investigator. For me, there has existed a line of demarcation between premeditated homicide and justifiable homicide. Often, that line has described the boundaries of love, honour, fidelity, and, yes, revenge. Across the boundary, however, there exists only savagery, cruelty, pathology, and horror. It has not been difficult for me to place myself on that line of demarcation on those occasions where the line was true and defined. My responsibility is to Reason. Atonement does not signify and is best left to those who practice in the realm of spiritual mythology.

13

Langdale Pike. A most extraordinary person. No one in London knew more about the gentry, the aristocracy or the Royals than Langdale Pike. He studied society as intensely as I studied crime. He organised and filed relationships, indiscretions, infidelities, affairs of the heart, addictions, bankruptcies—all the flotsam and jetsam of the upper class and the individual foibles of the most and least prominent of its members. This encyclopaedic knowledge was contained wholly within his formidable brain equipped with its photographic memory.

The workings of his mind were those of an automaton. A new fact stimulated a file of older facts and aligned them into new relevancies with other facts about other people pigeon-holed in perfect reason and deduction. Pike and I were equals operating in different disciplines, but using the same powers of observation, knowledge and synthesis.

Pike was born in London in 1855 to a wealthy family of long establishment in the law of admiralty, the insuring of vessels, and sole owners of a large shipping fleet. Through being the lawyers and the insurers, as well as the ships owners, their cases never went against themselves and, regardless of the verdict, the Pikes claimed either the reward or the fee. In consequence, the family amassed a fortune and ranked in the upper strata of London society.

Young Langdale went up to Cambridge where he studied the arts of the dilettante. His knowledge of fine art, porcelain, literature, music and theatre was sufficiently broad to equip him as a highly accomplished raconteur and favoured dinner quest. After coming down with an Ordinary in Humanities, Langdale took to spending his days at Swithin's, his club in St. James Street, lunching at the St. James Hotel where he daily sampled liberally the prize French wines in the hotel's extensive underground vaults, and returning to sit in Swithin's bow window to observe the to and fro movements of his specimens and be available to all who curried his favour by informing him of the latest gossip above and below stairs in the great homes of London society. Pike was created to be precisely what he was: a handsome mannequin, an arbiter of taste, and the repository of all of society's most intimate secrets. He was invaluable to me as a source of information, and I was invaluable to him as a source of hints and directions as to where to turn his energies.

Now, three years since his death, it is possible to accord Langdale Pike his proper place in history. London's most accomplished dilettante and gadfly was, in reality, Great Britain's most important intelligence officer from 1875 through his last years in the early 1920s. For nearly forty-five years, Pike filtered the endless river of gossip and innuendo that came his way daily and sieved from it those national and international bits and bobs that signalled threats to the monarchy, the government, and the people of Great Britain, passing them on to his one contact in Whitehall: Mycroft.

During the Great War, Pike was the human dial upon the surface of war. He alone was privy to the sacrifices and heroisms of the British upper class, as well as their perfidies, acts of treason and war profiteering. Masterfully inhabiting his well-developed role as social gadfly, Pike was instrumental in successfully forestalling forty-seven national threats to my certain knowledge and there may well be numerous others of which I am unaware. Only Mycroft knew for sure, and Mycroft was a closed book.

My intersections with Pike notably occurred in the business of the Bruce-Partington plans, and that of the naval treaty, the Greek interpreter, the red circle, Mrs Mary Maberly and, of course, the matter concerning Baron Von Herling. Not once in all the years was Pike ever wrong in his analyses or conclusions.

Langdale Pike was an example of what can emerge when privilege, wealth, education and class combine to benefit society. Just as easily, he could have been exactly what he seemed to be, but he wasn't. In many ways, like me, the Langdale Pike known to the world was partially a figment. Only through the successes of his work did we catch a glimpse of the real man.

14

Many of my cases were associated with America or had American connexions. I do not prefer Americans as their lack of education makes them difficult to penetrate. One has to work so hard to get to the truth with Americans and, then, it is often not to be relied upon. I admit to my having a definite prejudice for things British. Consequently, I was annoyed with Watson's insistence in devoting so much of his efforts to the Mormon case and the minor piece about the Scowrers. I have always thought the Pinkerton's to be amateurs in the business of crime detection and to devote two lengthy works to these cases was, in my opinion, a reflection of the publisher's wishes, or those of Watson's supposedly informed literary agent. I would have preferred a bit more of a focus on those cases where the highest levels of reasoning and deduction were demonstrated. One such early case where Watson accompanied me and kept excellent notes would have been the case of the vanished mayor of

Stow-on-the-Wold. One moment the mayor was in the chair presiding over the town council and in the blink of an eye he had vanished. The following fortnight was filled with the most intense period of reasoning I have ever been called upon to undertake. At the conclusion of the case my intellectual powers and reserves were at the lowest ebb of my career, then or since. The combinations of possibilities in that case would have required a two-volume edition to do justice to the complexities of the intellectual problems.

Even had Watson written of the Cotswold mayoral case, there can be no doubt whatsoever that the unparalleled mystery of the Avebury church crypt and dovecote showed powers of extrapolation and inferential observation to a degree never found in any other of my cases. Were I to sit down and simply list the chain of deductive tests that formed the basis for the premise and thence the proof, the number of pages would exceed three-hundred easily.

With the time required for Watson to write and negotiate for publication *A Study in Scarlet* and *The Valley of Fear*, he had no time to finish the eight extraordinary cases that we referred collectively to as "The Scotland Adventures." These were:

1. The McDonald of Skye and the missing sporran;

2. The blank gravestones of the Black Isle;

3. The Laird of MacCull and the Peruvian arrow;

4. The Hebridean magpie;

5. The Duke of Argyll's bloody leather kilt;

6. The Ness Walk amputee;

7. The shrinking whisky distillery;

8. The crone of Portree.

All of these cases presented far more interesting problems than my two concerning America. Perhaps I should next write fully of the Scotland adventures as I believe it is an important body of my work that should be available to serious students of crime and deduction. The events surrounding the Hebridean magpie and the astonishingly evil crone of Portree would occupy both criminologists and those who study the criminally insane for decades to come. Indeed, the crone is unique among all female antagonists of my experience.

Unknown to the world, and revealed for the first time in this brief but fascinating recounting of my life, I did travel to America and Mexico a second time after my 1912 trip as Altamont. It was in 1917, at the request of President Wilson, to obtain the infamous Zimmermann Telegram sent by the German Foreign Minister to the President of Mexico inviting Mexico to join Germany as an ally against the United States. In return, Germany would finance Mexico's war and help it recover the desolate territories of Texas, New Mexico and Arizona. After two weeks in Mexico City and a carefully arranged espionage plan, the telegram was delivered by a presidential palace valet to a coffee buyer from New Orleans and hidden inside a sack of green Arabica coffee beans from Chiapas. The coffee buyer set sail with his diplomatically sensitive cargo for New Orleans and within ten days personally handed the Zimmermann Telegram to President Wilson. Soon after the sinking of seven American merchant ships by the Germans, President Wilson revealed the Zimmermann Telegram to the American public and called for war on Germany, which the American Congress declared on 6 April 1917. The coffee buyer quietly returned to London and his familiar rooms in Montague Street, having made his last trip to North America.

15

Upon reading Watson's extensive notes, I am amused by the attention paid to restaurants, food, wine and spirits. He wrote sparingly of gastronomy in his books, but his notebooks are full of details of dinners we had together in restaurants and our rooms, as well as tasting notes on wines we shared which are found in a quite remarkable tasting journal I never knew he kept. Apparently, Watson had quite an unseen side to his personality.

The two of us dined often at Simpson's-in-the-Strand and I continue to have dinner there twice weekly, usually on Tuesday's and Friday's. Simpson's opened its doors in 1828 and has served traditional British food with few changes to the menu. The Grand Divan, Simpson's formal dining room, is a dark mahogany room with massive crystal chandeliers where comfort, excellent waiters and fine Scottish beef served from domed silver trolleys have been the tradition for over a century and a half. Its cellars house the grand and premier crus wines of the great chateaux of Bordeaux and the Burgundy vintages are of the highest quality and age. My favourites over the years have been the roast Scottish beef, the Scottish salmon and the saddle of lamb. Watson usually chose the excellent steak and kidney pie or the Dover sole. On occasion, after returning to London on an early morning train, we would go to Simpson's for the Great British Breakfast which has been unchanged since the restaurant's early beginning. We would have our fill of Cumberland sausages, streaky and back bacon, Stornoway black pudding, fried mushrooms, baked tomato and poached or fried eggs, as well as toast and orange marmalade and pots of hot tea or coffee. Watson was a tea man in the morning; I preferred coffee.

It was rare that Watson or I took lunch, although an ample tea at half-four each afternoon was looked to by Mrs Hunter. Her teas were quite splendid and our Scotland Yard friends often found good reasons to call for advice between four and half-four in expectation of her almond macaroons and orange cream pudding. Her breakfasts and dinners were quite good and she was always ready to see to our nourishment upon our arrival at any hour of the day or night. She still prepares tea today, but the housekeeper sees to light breakfasts and lunches and a few favourite dishes for our respective dinners.

Watson and I also dined at Christopher's at Number 18 Wellington Street, Covent Garden on occasion. The restaurant opened in an old papier maché factory and a casino was added in 1870. Watson made far too many racing bets from Christopher's as it was a centre for gaming in the last quarter of the century.

Another of our occasional haunts was Langbourn's Coffee House in Ball-Alley, Lombard Street. Rebuilt in 1850, it had a broiling-stove in the coffee-room, from whence chops and steaks were served hot from the gridiron around the clock. Langbourn's also had a wine and cigar room, embellished in a handsome old French décor. This was also one of my stops when I was intent on a case and needed only the necessities of nourishment: a glass of claret, a bit of cheese, and the rejuvenation of a good Cuban cigar.

My own taste runs to French cuisine, doubtless the influence of my mother and her preference for the dishes of Belgium, France and the grand resorts of Europe. When on my own, I would often have dinner at Rouget's in Castle Street, Leicester Square, where the French dishes were capitally done and the soup Julienne was as good as any to be had in London. Rouget's also had the advantages of being inexpensive and quiet. Unfortunately, it closed in 1900.

Whenever Watson and I required balm for our souls, we sought out Bertollini's in St. Martin's Place at the back of Pall Mall East. A wonderful man was Bertollini: a short heavily-built Ligurian from Recco on the Italian Riviera, who superintended every aspect of the restaurant himself: now instructing the kitchen; now decanting the wine; now pointing at table with his short fleshy fore-finger to especially succulent pieces in the dish. There is no doubt the ingredients were mysterious; but they were well-flavoured, well-seasoned, and always relished by me and by Watson. With a bottle of Chablis or Claret, Bertollini's food was a pleasant interlude from the roasted joint or the never-to-be-avoided chop to which the London tavern-diner was eternally condemned. Bertollini passed from life in 1910 and his restaurant was ceremoniously closed upon the closing of his coffin.

Watson enjoyed his whisky, never to excess, but well-appreciated after a long day at his surgery or after a longer night on the moors during one of our adventures. We maintained a small stock of vintage wines below stairs at Montague Street. Our wine and spirits merchant was Josiah Vamberry until his murder in the cellar of his establishment in Fleet Street. He was found badly corked with a wine key screwed into his brain and the word 'trahi' scratched into his forehead. I quickly connected the murder to two unsavoury characters in the employ of one 'Archison' who was implicated in a vast European conspiracy to destroy the French wine trade. The mysterious and deadly Archison was linked to a chateau in Margaux unexplainably owned by an obscure stationmaster in the West of England. Any connexion to Vamberry could not be established, but I remain steadfast in my belief of Moriarty's involvement. Regardless, we provided our spirits and wine custom thereafter to Francis

Davy in the Strand beginning in 1870, who continues to supply my fine wine needs today.

16

At the outset of this reflection, I stated that it was my intent to expand upon Watson' masquerades and inaccuracies found in his body of writings about our years together. When one reads the various stories, one is given Holmes through Watson, and Watson is often generous to Holmes to a fault.

There exist a number of textual and factual inaccuracies, created intentionally by Watson, that portray me in a more favourable light. Ever my Boswell, Watson sought always to put me at the heroic centre of the stories (how I abhor that word; these are historical, scientific archives, not 'stories' which imply fictions). I cannot allow these untruths to endure and, here, will set but three to rights, although there are fifty-six other instances of intentional inaccuracy in the entire written collection.

In the matter of Silver Blaze, Watson's text has me replying to Gregory's question, 'Is there any point to which you would wish to draw my attention?' with the words, 'To the curious incident of the dog in the night-time.' Gregory retorted, 'The dog did nothing in the night-time.' I supposedly re-joined with, 'That was the curious incident.'

The truth, in fact, was quite different. Watson had been particularly acute during our investigations at Dartmoor. More than once, he had surprised me with connexions that imparted insights to my findings. I had specifically asked Watson for his impressions and insights on the case and his reasoning was quite beyond his normal performance. During our walk across the moor, when we reached the hollow and I remarked with a bit of smugness to Watson, 'See the value of imagination' he came out of his reverie, looked at me and said, 'But, Holmes, what about the curious incident of the dog in the night-time?' It was I who replied, 'The dog did nothing in the night-time' and it was Watson who penetrated to the truth asking, 'Was that not a curious incident, Holmes?' From there, I made immediate inferences leading to proofs, and we know the outcome. But good old Watson went to some pains to write the narrative in a way that deflected the flash of deductive brilliance from him, placing it entirely upon me.

A second moment of prescient illumination visited Watson during the case involving Sir Robert Norberton and our investigations in Berkshire. It occurred at the Green Dragon when Watson and I were considering the data surrounding the supposedly curious behaviour of Lady Beatrice Falder. My own preferences favoured only Sir Robert's imminent bankruptcy as the motive for his deceitful actions. However, it was Watson who reasoned the importance of the crypt and Lady Beatrice's devoted dog and returned to that point several times, finally suggesting to me that Lady Beatrice may have died and been placed secretly in the crypt. Once again, it was Watson's insight that gave me the final piece of data necessary to order the logic and complete the deductions needed to solve the Shoscombe Old Place case. As true as the unvarying constellation he was, Watson wrote of the adventure in a way that once more positioned me as the pole star of the solution when, in truth, I can only accept partial credit.

Perhaps the greatest of Watson's intentional masquerades, however, is found in his writing of the case he called *The Adventure of the Blanched Soldier*. It is a manuscript ostensibly written under my own hand in response to Watson's retort, 'Try it yourself, Holmes' when I admonished him for his pandering to popular taste in his writing rather than confining himself rigidly to facts. In the long opening paragraph, I devote myself to a somewhat ungracious satirical account of Watson's 'remarkable characteristics' and demean his mind as a perpetual closed book. The quality of the writing is not up to that of Watson and my oft-repeated demand for a scientific archival approach to the cases and not a sensationalist spectacle is never achieved in the manuscript. And this is Watson's finest moment, his greatest score on me for all of my years of criticisms of his abilities, for the story was not written by me. It was written by Watson in my persona and its faux failure to achieve my own standards for writing is, singularly, Watson's finest moment. In recent years, with the modest success of Watson's books, quite a number of people from all levels of society—waiters, tradesmen, country squires, nobles, even monarchs—say to me, 'Your writing talents are superb, Mr Holmes' and 'You should really write more of your adventures,

Mr Holmes' or 'I do believe you missed out on a marvellous career as a writer, Mr Holmes.' The only thing I can say is, 'Thank you; I am sure you are overly kind' and, whenever I have done, I hear a soft, quiet laugh coming from Watson's favourite chair next the fireplace. Good old Watson.

꧁꧂

17

While I never wrote of my cases or career, I did, in 1925, complete the great work of my life: *The Science of Deduction and Detection*. The book is scheduled by the publisher to be introduced in mid-1930 to coincide with the celebration of the centenary of Scotland Yard. The work is in five volumes, each having three-hundred fifty pages. It was written over a period of eighteen years and is held as the authoritative treatment of the subject. The publisher is G. P. Putnam's Sons of London. I am confident of the work standing on its own and, doubtless, it may eclipse my apparent wide celebrity owing to the many sensationalist stories of Watson.

Other, specific works were completed and published throughout my career, and included:

1. *Upon the Distinction Between the Ashes of the Various Tobaccos;*

2. *Upon the Polyphonic Motets of Lassus;*

3. *Upon the Characteristics of Ears: Attachment and Structural Differences;*

4. *Upon the Characteristics of Ears: Lobuli Auricularum;*

5. *Upon the Subject of Secret Writings: An Analysis of One-Hundred-Sixty Ciphers;*

6. *Upon the Dating of Documents;*

7. *Upon Tattoos: Designs, Pigments and Methodologies;*

8. *Upon the Tracing of Footsteps: Shod;*

9. *Upon the Tracing of Footsteps: Unshod;*

10. *Upon the Influence of Trade upon Deformities of the Hand;*

11. *Upon Chaldean Roots of the Cornish Language;*

12. *Upon the Decomposition of Human Tissues.*

All of the monographs except for that concerning Lassus were translated into French by François le Villard and subsequently published in a single-volume by Bernhardt Tauchnitz of Leipzig. The Tauchnitz edition had reasonable reception in India and the Orient, but oddly is rarely found in Britain or America.

My most successful book—commercially—was *Practical Handbook of Bee Culture* which has sold well for its publisher, Hodder and Stoughton, Limited of London. By its containing many revolutionary observations and measurements never before recognized by even the most experienced apiasts, the book has altered forever the directions and practices of bee-keeping worldwide and has brought me, in consequence, handsome annual royalties. And, were it not for my celebrated book, the world would still be unaware of Royal Jelly and its beneficial properties, a discovery I am most proud of and pleased to have revealed.

18

I am grateful for the many recognitions of my talents that have come over the years. Even those of us who attempt self-effacement in deference to the official police investigators ask ourselves whether the world at large is aware of our small contributions to the betterment of society. I am reminded of a unique recognition that I was honoured to accept and that stands alone for its incorporation of my work with that of the greatest detectives of the world.

I was called to Bruxelles in September of 1901 at the invitation of les Compagnons de la Branche d'Or, the highly esteemed society of Europe's distinguished police detectives, to accept investiture as a Compagnon of this over one-hundred year old group of elites. La Branche d'Or members have, to their credit, solved the most difficult, most important cases in modern European history. Any of the twelve Compagnons are worthy of knighthood or equal honours for their superior service to their respective countries. In the annals of these twelve men, forty-nine plots of anarchy, treason and rebellion have been put down as a result of their near-mythic talents. It was truly a humbling experience to be invited to their ranks in recognition of my work in the case known as *The Naval Treaty*, which, had I not been successful, might have led to a prolonged, chaotic and, doubtless, bloody European instability.

Of all the Compagnons over the years, only two have come from the milieu of the private detective, all others being of the official police. I was the first private consulting detective invited and, twenty-five years later, a second, formerly of Belgium, was invested and I extended my respect and welcome to him during the annual ceremonies of 1926, the last I have attended. After my twenty-eight years as a Compagnon, I retired my ceremonial chapeau this year, making room for a new and younger member to be inducted into this honourable group of men who have done so much to keep the fabric of civilized society intact.

Other awards and recognitions have come from heads of state and monarchs of various countries where I made some small contribution. I have been presented with the badges of a number of Orders, Legions and Societies from across Europe, all gratefully accepted and added to the now sizeable collection in the tin biscuit box in my bedroom. While pleasant to contemplate, I must admit to a preference for more fungible rewards.

In recent years, several public structures have been named for me. One I particularly appreciate is a marble fountain in Russell Square designated the Sherlock Holmes Fountain and erected by a loyal friend and chivalrous gentlemen in appreciation for my somewhat painful services in the Baron Adelbert Gruner business. I have often observed the birds refreshing themselves in this small corner fountain, surrounded by red rose-bushes, with its tantalisingly unique carved decoration in the marble of a single ostrich feather supported with the Welsh motto, *Eich Dyn,* and thought to myself how much more appropriate it is than a garter or another badge with which I might have been honoured instead.

Another small, but favourite, recognition can be found in the Hotel Russell, just a short walk from 47 Montague Street, across Russell Square. Several years after the hotel was built in 1898, beginning in 1903, I came to enjoy an afternoon platter of fresh oysters and a pint of bitter in the hotel's Tempus Bar. For me, nothing quite fixes the digestion as two-dozen large oysters. It is now nearly twenty-six years later and I still take my almost daily afternoon stroll to the Tempus for my refreshment. The bar man, Stillwell, has been there since the hotel opened and is, in truth, one of my few regular acquaintances and confidants. He has caused to be affixed to my unchanging bar chair at the far end a brass plate engraved with 'Reserved In Perpetuity for Sherlock Holmes.' I find this to be, perhaps, the most gracious of all my recognitions.

At least three days of each week, I am joined at the Tempus Bar by an old client, now in his seventy-seventh year and still plying his old trade. Each clement day he comes very early from his home in Kent to his place of business in the shelter of the side door of the British Museum where he sells a few small goods and accepts the generosity of passers-by. Known for his wit and kind humour freely dispensed, he makes a most handsome annual turnover in this simple way. At a quarter four each afternoon, he bags his ample takings and meets me at the Russell where we take our refreshment and discuss the news of the day. He then departs for home, happily anticipating the company of his understanding wife. Known to the public as Hugh Boone, Mr Neville St. Claire had been at the centre of one of my more unusual cases in 1889. After its conclusion, he had repented of his mendicant ways and joined his family accountancy firm. Quickly tiring of the dull routine of the counting house, he convinced his wife that he could do better financially and be far happier by returning to his old persona as Hugh Boone, the unfortunate beggar who brings laughter and gayety to the daily audience of passers-by who value his blithe spirit and cheerfully reward him with bags of silver coins.

St. Clair's two sons have been educated at Eton and Oxford and are highly successful; one in medicine and one in the law. Mrs St. Clair has, over the years, perfected the beauty of their country estate and often welcomes their four grandchildren for long, summer visits.

St. Clair regularly stops by my rooms for a fast-paced game of chess, and over the intervening years we have exercised our brains together and became friends.

He remains the most singularly unique individual of my knowledge, and he has been a fine husband, father and stimulating afternoon companion.

As each year passes, I sense the looming reality of impermanence. For all of the powers I bring to my profession, ultimately they dissipate in time and memory and one day are forgotten entirely. The most one can hope for is a small plaque somewhere, a bit of eternal marble, or a few books in an obscure library archiving a few cases that revealed a few brief moments of excellence; to hope for more is futile in a complex and crowded world.

19

For nearly a year my nemesis was Mrs Adele Turner. She was Mrs Hunter's mother's sister, a widow and an unfortunate woman who would break the patience of the dead. She joined the Arbuthnot household in 1888 as a cook, but her culinary ability was so poor that she was soon moved to the position as maid and Mrs Hunter took over the cook's duties as well as her own as housekeeper. Having her aunt under her was difficult, but then everything about Mrs Turner was difficult. She had been married to the captain of a coastal schooner, sailing with him wherever his trade took him, and she was all Bristol shape and unbearable with her clean and neat shipboard ways.

As a maid becalmed in Bloomsbury, Mrs Turner made it her chief duty to keep our rooms organised, tidy and spotless. My instructions went unheeded; Mr Arbuthnot had neither influence over nor even awareness of Mrs Turner. Her niece, who was purportedly in charge of the household, was wholly unable to direct her forty-three year old aunt in any regard. In short, my world was a shambles. Watson was in practice in Paddington and was not in residence during that *annus horribilis*.

Each morning commenced with the airing of the rooms, the infernal 'tricing up' and the tidying of all surfaces. I detest fresh air in the morning; I detest tidying; only my mind is tidy; the rest of my surroundings must be functional for my purposes, requiring a certain degree of bestiality. My chemical experiments must mature, or ferment, or precipitate; they cannot be scrubbed and tidied about. My tobacco plugs and dottles are *meant* to dry on the mantelpiece, not to be swept into the dust bin with a 'cluck-cluck' sound of the tongue. My commonplace books and newspapers are kept in an order known only to me and at hand on the floor at the side of my chair; they are not to be stacked neatly or arranged properly on a shelf in another room. My correspondence is kept in my ordained order on the mantel by penetration with a knife; it is not alphabetised and pigeon-holed by date in the secretary. My linens, my collars, my shirts, my bed-clothes are all of my personal domain and are not to be 'freshened' or 'done-up' or any other such bothersome interference; I want no one to 'do' for me. And, a gentleman's rooms require a proper patina of living; the constant smell of carbolic soap is anathema and reminds one of why Turkish baths can only be tolerated once a fortnight.

During that year, I instructed Wiggins to bring the entire corps of Irregulars to my rooms three times a week, preferably with meat pies for which I gratefully passed out shillings to buy in order to vanquish the enforced sterility and barrenness of freshly-washed woodwork.

The final insult came during a case involving Carlos Estoya Esteban, the Spanish mortician, in which it was necessary for me to dissect dozens of Thames eels to look for evidence of the disposal over time of a number of dead bodies in the tidal flats above The Pool. Mrs Turner, in her daily fit of indignation, did away with essential digestive evidence that would have put Esteban in prison for life. From that moment, I resolved to loose myself from the clutches of this bothersome drudge of the high seas.

In 1887, I had encountered Mordecai Smith during the Sholto affair and had felt a degree of compassion for the small-time bargeman and his family of unfortunates. When Jonathon Small was captured and Smith and his son were taken into custody, I quietly arranged with Athelney Jones for leniency as regarded Smith. The master of the *Aurora* was in my debt and I made a call upon him at his wharf to collect my principal and interest.

Within three days a handsome ship's captain nearing fifty years of age, located, arranged for and contracted by Smith and financed by me, called at Montague Street, inquiring for Mrs Adele Turner. He said he had known her husband and was aware of her years of service sailing with him to ports as far away as the Mediterranean. He offered her a berth on his cutter bound for the East as ship's cook and purser with her own quarters at a tenth share of the profits, a sum that was worth over three-hundred a year, an all but unheard of offer in the sailing trade. With her shipboard ways, her desire to return to the life she had loved, and the added potential of a handsome and unmarried captain to work under, Mrs Turner took herself and her box off to the docks within two days.

Life at 47 Montague Street returned to normal: Mrs Hunter regained her pleasant smile; Mr Arbuthnot had no idea what had occurred; and I was again in control of my world, my environment and my life.

Mrs Turner left London on a long trading voyage to the Japans early in the spring aboard the cutter *Alicia*. One can only assume she found her proper place, at sea beyond the mist.

20

Mercer. Watson mentioned him only once in the writing and he is nowhere to be found in Watson's extensive notes. The reason for this thin treatment is that Watson and Mercer did not get along.

Watson dismisses Mercer's earlier presence in my cases by having me state, 'Mercer is since your time,' which was not entirely correct. Watson was attempting to make his own valued association more keenly felt by me and, therefore, he sought to lessen the importance of any other member of my corps of agents. To be entirely fair to Watson, he was of great assistance to me in most of my cases, but he was not my only assistant.

My early association with William Mercer came about in 1873 while I was at university. A fellow student, Victor Trevor, invited me to his family home at Donnithorpe, in Norfolk, where his father, the local J. P., lived alone. In consequence of a few of my observational inferences regarding his father, the visit became the first case in which I was ever engaged.

In the narrative recounting the events at sea in 1855 written by Trevor senior—who was in reality one James Armitage—he tells the bloody history of the *Gloria Scott* and of the escape of five convicts and three sailors when Jack Prendergast, a transported convict who had taken over the vessel and murdered most of the crew and guards, relented and allowed the eight to take a boat and leave the ship at Lat. 15° and Long 25° west. The narrative accounts for Prendergast's killing of the captain, the third mate, the doctor, the warders, and all others loyal to the ship. It does not, however, account for the second mate, but it does state that *three* sailors escaped in the boat. One of the three was, in fact, the second mate who, as Prendergast's acknowledged right-hand man, had repudiated Pendergast's mass killing and had, at great danger of being murdered himself as a traitor, convinced Prendergast to spare their lives and set them adrift.

The second mate was rescued along with the others, as well as the seaman Hudson who survived the explosion that took the *Gloria Scott* to the bottom, by the brig *Hotspur,* and James Armitage—who owed the third mate his life for standing up to Prendergast and securing their freedom— befriended the sailor and, along with Evans, ultimately made their way to the Australian gold fields, where all three disappeared, changed their names, became wealthy and years later returned to England as rich colonials and bought country estates. Trevor senior's real name was, as we know, James Armitage; Beddoes real name was Evans; and the third mate, who changed his name to William Mercer, was really Walter Mereer. His second mate's papers were in the name of W. Mereer and, because of the way the second 'e' had been hand-engrossed, it was quite easily altered to a 'c' and his identity changed.

Mereer, now Mercer, came to Donnithorpe with Trevor senior and, being wealthy in his own right, purchased a comfortable house on property between Trevor senior's estate and that of a neighbour, Sir Edward Holly, where he pursued an interest and trade in Ancient English Manorial Deeds.

When the truth of the case emerged, he approached me and revealed all that his old friend Trevor senior had left unstated in his narrative. When I was convinced of his having committed no act of murder aboard the *Gloria Scott* and his intercession resulting in the saving of seven lives, I agreed to leave any conclusions to the official police who were unaware of either

Mereer or Mercer and were only peripherally interested in the closure of the cases of the missing Beddoes and Hudson.

In appreciation and owing to a desire to leave the past behind, Mercer turned his singular talents for research and routine investigation from ancient deeds to the far more interesting investigations of Sherlock Holmes. He moved to London and took rooms in Baker Street where he devoted at least two days a week to my requirements for data, research, confidential investigation, and anonymous errands and arrangements. He was a valuable and able assistant and was in my employ as Agent from 1874 to 1910 when, at the ripe age of eighty, he passed away. Watson did not accompany me to his funeral.

21

Sufficient time has passed for me to now reveal the fact that Charles Augustus Milverton was not Charles Augustus Milverton. In 1889, the man who would be Milverton had earlier adopted that name upon his return to England after ten years of collecting the intimate and indiscreet secrets of European and British nobility and those of the wealthiest members of society to use as a perpetual source of foul income from blackmail. I considered him to be the worst man in London, not only for his crimes but for the utter blackness of his heart.

My first encounter with the man to be known as Milverton had occurred in 1888, the year before he fled England after the treachery involving Mr Melas, the Greek interpreter. I had never come face-to-face with him until 1899, knowing of his earlier treachery only through an accomplice who had responsibility for the death of the son and the kidnapping of the daughter of an immensely wealthy Greek family. With a fortune in ransom, having absconded to Budapest, he killed both his initial accomplice in murder and kidnapping, Harold Latimer, and a second accomplice with whom he switched identities and papers after also stabbing him to death. The second accomplice was the actual Charles Augustus Milverton, a card-sharp from Plymouth who made his living in the casinos of Athens and Istanbul and who had come into acquaintance with Paul Kratides. Using the ransom money and Milverton's identity, the murderer and kidnapper embarked on a new life of society blackmail on the continent. His real name was Wilson Kemp.

The daughter of the prominent Greek family was Sophy Kratides, and it was Sophy Kratides, the beautiful and wealthy member of Athens and London society, who had, in 1897, married the Marquess of Roehampton. He subsequently died of a broken heart two years later when Milverton sent him letters from a previous lover of his wife when she refused to see Milverton again, remembering the horror of her poor brother's kidnaping and death.

Sophy Kratides Beauchamp, Marchioness of Roehampton, was the veiled lady who emptied barrel after barrel into Milverton's chest, ground her heel into his face, and avenged her noble husband's death and the broken spirits of so many other women the foul Latimer had brutalised.

Watson captured my position perfectly regarding the disposition of the case when I gave Lestrade my summary:

> 'Well, I'm afraid I can't help you, Lestrade. The fact is that I knew this fellow Milverton, that I considered him one of the most dangerous men in London, and I think there are certain crimes which the law cannot touch, and which therefore, to some extent, justify private revenge.'

Another blackmailer, equally devoid of human value as Milverton, was masqueraded by Watson in an 1894 case. It was only through the most assiduous unravelling of the multiple threads placing this blackmailer at the centre of a massive web extending back and forth across the Continent that I was able to put the matter to rights and relieve the tensions that had threatened the highest levels of the British government with the certainty of impending war. My subversive restoration of Trelawney Hope's missing letter was, perhaps, the one moment where I changed the history of Great Britain and, indeed, possibly the lives of a hundred thousand of our bravest men, by averting the precipice of a malformed destiny. But, the story written as *The Adventure of the Second Stain* does not tell quite all that occurred and deserves further explanation.

Eduardo Lucas and Henri Fournaye were one and the same. The Lucus persona was known to me, in that he numbered among the three well-known London conduits of international intrigue-for-profit. The Fournaye persona had not made his way into my notice, as his work was carried out in Paris and was concentrated in the Gypsy enclaves for which I had little interest. It is possible that other personas and blackmail specialties existed in other cities for this master criminal prior to his death, although none have, as yet, emerged in the criminal record. Inquiries led me to conclude that Lucas and Fournaye were each aliases used by an unknown but brilliant criminal who moved easily between his various bases of operations and his various disguised personas until he was killed by Mme Fournaye, the woman said to be his Creole wife, in their villa in Rue Austerlitz, Paris.

When Mme Fournaye was returned briefly from Paris to London to be closely questioned about her role in the international web that had shaken the highest reaches of British rule, I ascertained through careful questioning and observations of her physical responses that Henri Fournaye may not have been her husband's real name. When she admitted to his having been married previously, I pressed her for the details of that earlier wife. She related to me the following facts:

1. Fournaye only spoke of his first wife on two occasions and each time mentioned her name as being Mary.

2. A letter was found by Mme Fournaye from Lucy Parr with Streatham in the inscription. The salutation is simply 'Dear Miss Mary' and goes on to ask Mary's return home citing the seriousness of her uncle's health.

That was all that Mme Fournaye knew about her husband's first marriage, and she could give no information as to his possible identity. She had met him in Paris when she immigrated from Jamaica and had only known him as Henri Fournaye. They were married in common law. She passed from my knowledge into a French prison, convicted of the murder of Henri Fournaye, to spend the remainder of her days.

The letter from Lucy Parr, found in the Fournaye household, led to a number of connexions whereby I concluded that Henri Fournaye's first wife was, in fact, Mary Holder, the adopted niece of Alexander Holder whose son Arthur's reputation I had salvaged in the beryl coronet case during December of 1890. Mary Holder was lost to her family as a consequence of her unfortunate infatuation with the villainous and contemptible Sir George Burnwell with whom she had disappeared. And Sir George Burnwell had moved on from theft to society blackmail in his adopted serial identities as Eduardo Lucas, Henri Fournaye and, doubtless, many others.

One can only reflect that, when I had clapped a pistol to this blackguard's temple in 1890, perhaps I should have saved England then from the dangerous future progression of this singularly amoral individual's growing ambition that would metastasise to treason in only four short years.

I mention aspects from these cases to underscore once again the necessary balance that must be present when justice is properly served. As I look back on my career, I do not hear myself saying, 'I wish I had been more detached,' nor do I hear myself saying, 'I wish I had been more compassionate.' I find myself accepting what has been the sum and substance of my career: proper attention to the facts—cerebral and human—of each situation.

22

Inspector Ambrose Hill was unique in my experience of the Scotland Yard detectives. He was the first of the 'specialists' to emerge in the Metropolitan force beginning in the early 1890s. The specialists were both vertical and horizontal; that is, vertical as to criminal communities, such as nationalities, classes of society, area of focus such as banking, art, real property, and others; and horizontal as to the categories of crimes, such as murder, robbery, forgery, kidnapping and their ilk. At its fullest expansion, the specialist ranking had inspectors who focused, for example, only on murders in the Chinese quarter or embezzlement in the banking sector, or theft and counterfeiting of fine art. It proved to be a more efficient manner of utilisation of what little there was of available skill and talent.

Inspector Hill was a thrice-talented specialist: he concentrated on Saffron Hill, a small region near Hatton Garden; the Italian Quarter; and secret crime organisations like the Mafia. Hill was educated at University College London and intellectually was able to bridge from the upper to the immigrant classes. He spoke flawless Italian, read Greek and Latin, and was a formidable all-rounder on the cricket pitch with a near-impossible combination leg-break and googly. Hill lived on St. Cross Street between Saffron Hill and Kirby Street, thus having ready exposure to the criminal events of his surroundings.

I shall forever be deeply in debt to Inspector Hill for his near-obsessive work from November 1895 to the following November. This year-long, indefatigable investigation resulted in the solving of one of Saffron Hill's most unspeakable murders, a cesspool of horrors, and the vacating of erroneous charges against a member of my family.

During this missing year, my practice was all but suspended while I seconded Hill in uncovering the malevolent forces leading to the murder that ensnared an innocent, universally trusted and highly-placed member of the government. It was necessary for me to recuse myself to a great degree due to my unfortunate and wrongly accused relation; however, I provided Hill with an anchor chain firmly embedded in fact and reason to guide his investigations, and he came to the end a credit to himself and Scotland Yard.

Ambrose Hill retired from Scotland Yard soon after his lengthy battle with the Saffron Hill Murderer. He found light, warm breezes and his love of the Italian aesthetic in a small villa in Tuscany, on a hillside not far from Florence, overlooking a tiny valley where his vineyard produces some of Italy's finest wine. He was a great friend to me, a rarely talented detective, a brave and good man, and he deserves a life of peace, joy and contentment, for he provided a great service in clearing the name of an innocent man in that terrible year.

During the summer of 1895, another case called me away from London for two months. I was summoned by the Bishop of Urgell, co-prince of the Principality of Andorra, bordering on Spain and France in the Pyrenees mountains, to solve a mysterious case involving a highly-placed Papal emissary that threatened the peaceful mountain state. With a population of just over five thousand, Andorra relied on sheep for its economy along with an active trade in the blending and rolling of cigars for European tastes. The tiny country's language and temperament is Catalan, and the Catalan ways are reflected throughout the culture.

The principality is predominately Roman Catholic. In Andorran lore, on the sixth of January during a year in the late twelfth century, a wild rose was found blooming out of season by villagers from Meritxell walking to mass in Canillo. At the base of the rose was a statue of the Virgin and Child. The statue was placed in the Canillo church, but was found the next day under the same rose bush. Next, the statue was taken to the church in Encamp. However, it was found again under the same rose bush the next day. The villagers took this as a sign and built a new chapel at the site of the rose bush in Meritxell and, in time, the Church in Rome elevated one of the women who found the statue and was present at several miracles over the years to sainthood and she became Meritxell, the patron saint of Andorra. The Prelate of Andorra was Cardinal Tosca who was also the Vatican Treasurer from 1880 to the time of the occurrences in this case.

The Bishop of Urgell in his official role as co-prince had hosted Cardinal Tosca at a dinner attended by one Juan Arnau of Caboet, Viscount of Castellbo, a descendant of one of Andorra's most noble families and its principal banker. The Viscount's daughter, Ermessenda Fernét, Countess Foix, was also present with her French husband, Epare Fernét, the Count of Foix. It was a tradition of the Andorran nobility to marry with the French nobility, thus maintaining the long Catalan and French stability and control.

During dinner, the Bishop of Urgell gave Cardinal Tosca an ornate casket containing a relic of Saint Meritxell, five bones of her right foot, the foot that when set upon a trailside rock of the Les Bons Valley between the villages of Encamp and Meritxell caused the snow to melt instantly across the entire valley and rose bushes to simultaneously burst into bloom, one of her several miracles of seven-hundred years earlier. The casket and its sacred bones were a gift to be conveyed by Cardinal Tosca to the Pope in Rome from whom Urgell hoped to obtain favour and receive the Papal imprimatur for Andorran cigars which was held, at that time, by Havana. The sizable appetite for premium cigars within the Vatican would measurably improve the lives of all Andorrans and earn Urgell a modest but permanent commission for his intercession with the Holy See.

The next morning before breakfast, Cardinal Tosca, who was a guest of the Bishop of Urgell at the Andorran palace, rushed to the Bishop's chapel where he was in early morning prayer. The Cardinal related the startling news that, overnight, the saint's foot has disappeared from the casket. Upon retiring the previous evening, Tosca has carried the casket with him to his suite and had opened it and looked upon the revered foot before locking it into a chest in his room. Upon awakening, he found a wild red rose upon the chest. Immediately, he unlocked the wood chest, withdrew the casket, opened it, and found that the sacred foot of Saint Meritxell had disappeared.

The Bishop of Urgell, horrified by the loss and alternately hopeful that another miracle had occurred, launched a full investigation but to no avail. Cardinal Tosca returned to Rome, empty-handed but with suspicion regarding Epare Fernét, Count of Foix, whom the Cardinal believed to be an enemy of the church. After several weeks, an envoy of the Pope, a simple Irish priest, was sent to London to request that I quietly look into the disappearance of the sacred relic. Apparently, the loss of the sainted foot was either too great or its potential use after recovery even greater for even the Pope to ignore.

Over the next fortnight, stemming from information provided me by my Irish priest envoy from Rome, my investigations extended to the official and unofficial church accounts of missing Catholic relics in other European countries. In none of these instances was any connection to the Count of Foix found, nor was there any connection with Cardinal Tosca, the Bishop of Urgell, the Viscount of Castellbo, or his daughter. The foot of Saint Meritxell was but one of fifteen holy relics to be missing in the last two years. Not only was the Pope's concern justified, but he suspected that an organized plot was afoot to steal the most sacred and revered relics of the church.

I visited Paris the following week and called upon the Count of Foix and his wife. While loyal to the church, they suggested that I look into rumoured recent losses in the accounts of the Vatican treasury, headed by Cardinal Tosca, information that had surfaced from bankers involved with the Count's family holdings. They both suggested that the Cardinal was not to be trusted and that he had begun to discredit the Count and Countess at the highest levels of the Holy See in order to discredit their speaking out against him.

The Irish priest, having direct access to the Pope, secretly began an examination of the church treasury where he discovered fourteen incidents of unexplained shortages that were subsequently covered with unexplained deposits. The Papal diary which has entries of all the movements of all Cardinals and envoys showed me that, during the week of each shortage being recorded in the accounts, Cardinal Tosca was within a half-day's travel to the location of a sacred relic when it was reported missing.

Confronted with my facts and conclusions, Tosca admitted to the Pope that he was taking money from the treasury and replacing it with money from the sale of the sacred relics to religious, fanatic collectors. He had grown rich by impoverishing the church. Within a month, Tosca and his name were stricken from the history of the church and he was declared *excomunicato* and *anathema* by the Pope, sent forever into the darkness.

Within another fortnight, the Irish envoy had contacted each of the fourteen collectors and persuaded them to make an appropriate donation to the church in lieu of their eternal damnation by the Pope or, at the very least, imprisonment for receiving stolen goods. In consequence of those fears, all fourteen of the relics were restored. Only the last one, the foot of Meritxell, was never found. But, on the site where the casket once was kept, at the church built to honour Saint Meritxell, a wild rose bush was found growing outside the door of the church. It blooms with only one rose year-round, a rose that the local Andorrans, a people for whom the supernatural comes naturally, say never dies.

23

On each of the few occasions in my life when I have spoken with someone informally and not about a case, the topic of politics presents itself to some degree or other. I detest politics and as a rule do not go wading in that stagnant pond.

It is not from ignorance of the workings or the potentials of political activity that I avoid involvement in political subjects or situations. It is because I can see no utility in politics. It is not an efficient method of either solving problems or providing services. Politics principally involves power, favour, money and influence, and those all lead inevitably to corruption of purpose and not to efficiency of solutions.

Whether I am a monarchist is immaterial. Neither a monarchy nor a parliamentarian form of government can result in truth or an accurate assessment of the necessary actions that will result in the proper benefits for all people.

Nations, in my opinion, can only be organised on an equally distributive form of social benefit. That is, nations must care for their people equally without respect of class, wealth, education, or other rankings. As a practical way of organizing societies, such an ideal is impossible and, therefore, does not interest me.

All politicians can do is offer up to the public reasons for according them power based on perceived reciprocal benefits. One politician attempts favour by offering better wages, and preaches a doctrine of 'economic expansion.' Another offers favour by restricting wages and calls it 'economic reform.' Both fail to arrive at the truth or an accurate solution to the problem. The time, energy and resources expended to contest the two erroneous positions are wholly wasted.

My study of crime has demonstrated that the origination of crime is in 'getting.' Criminals are essentially getting or taking something from someone else, from money to a life. Remove the desire or necessity to 'get' and crime would stop. Organise society in a manner where 'getting' is not required and many of our criminal problems will disappear. Even passionate crimes, such as murder, are, by and large, due to a passion for obtaining something, often relief from jealousy, revenge, hatred, anger and fear. Remove these stimuli and murderous responses decline.

As has been pointed out at some length, my knowledge of disciplines other than crime, chemistry and deduction is limited. Therefore, I have seldom spent time finding either questions or answers in other realms. Like the organisation of the planets and the sun, I am content to leave politics to others, although I despair of its being left in the hands of politicians.

Similarly, I find myself in much the same position regarding religion. Those who believe find it impossible to question or doubt; and those who doubt find it impossible to rely on faith. Non-believers reason based on scientific refutation; believers parrot based on supernatural acceptance. Neither can observe and synthesize from or to the truth. Therefore, it is an impossible position and one in which I have no interest.

Distilled to their essence, politics should embody equality and religion should embody truths of Nature. In both cases, I have my own conclusions.

24

At this late date, I see no reason to continue my long opaqueness regarding Moriarty's informer, Fred Porlock, who brought my attention to the Birlstone case.

Porlock was highly placed in the Moriarty web. He was one of a very few who received his instructions from Moriarty directly, a sign of trust from the master and a position to be granted only after years of repeated testing. Of course, no one was ever fully trusted by Moriarty who maintained his empire through fear and final retribution for those who failed him.

Like most of Moriarty's agents, Porlock was a simple man essentially faceless in the human parade of London. He was European but had lived in England for many years. He spoke flawless English and easily passed as a native of London. He had worked in a number of the best hotels and had come to Moriarty's notice when he was a waiter at the Grosvenor, a favourite of Moriarty's for its excellent food.

Initially, Porlock was employed as a valet to Moriarty and travelled with him throughout Europe as body-man to the mathematician, although initially he had no knowledge of Moriarty's criminal activities. As he became trusted, he was given periodic tasks conducting messages and instructions to the lower layers of Moriarty's organisation. As he tested true, he was slowly advanced in rank until he became involved as an accessory to such a degree that he was thereafter in thrall to Moriarty who ultimately came to possess his soul.

Porlock had a son who he had raised in Europe after his wife died giving birth. His son was unaware of the true nature of his father's work and Porlock had been diligent about keeping Moriarty from ever reaching into his son's life. That desire for good may have been the goad that moved him to act as an informer and often relief from jealousy, revenge, hatred, anger and fear. Remove these stimuli and murderous responses decline.

As has been pointed out at some length, my knowledge of disciplines other than crime, chemistry and deduction is limited. Therefore, I have seldom spent time finding either questions or answers in other realms. Like the organisation of the planets and the sun, I am content to leave politics to others, although I despair of its being left in the hands of politicians.

Similarly, I find myself in much the same position regarding religion. Those who believe find it impossible to question or doubt; and those who doubt find it impossible to rely on faith. Non-believers reason based on scientific refutation; believers parrot based on supernatural acceptance. Neither can observe and synthesize from or to the truth. Therefore, it is an impossible position and one in which I have no interest.

Distilled to their essence, politics should embody equality and religion should embody truths of Nature. In both cases, I have my own conclusions.

24

At this late date, I see no reason to continue my long opaqueness regarding Moriarty's informer, Fred Porlock, who brought my attention to the Birlstone case.

Porlock was highly placed in the Moriarty web. He was one of a very few who received his instructions from Moriarty directly, a sign of trust from the master and a position to be granted only after years of repeated testing. Of course, no one was ever fully trusted by Moriarty who maintained his empire through fear and final retribution for those who failed him.

Like most of Moriarty's agents, Porlock was a simple man essentially faceless in the human parade of London. He was European but had lived in England for many years. He spoke flawless English and easily passed as a native of London. He had worked in a number of the best hotels and had come to Moriarty's notice when he was a waiter at the Grosvenor, a favourite of Moriarty's for its excellent food.

Initially, Porlock was employed as a valet to Moriarty and travelled with him throughout Europe as body-man to the mathematician, although initially he had no knowledge of Moriarty's criminal activities. As he became trusted, he was given periodic tasks conducting messages and instructions to the lower layers of Moriarty's organisation. As he tested true, he was slowly advanced in rank until he became involved as an accessory to such a degree that he was thereafter in thrall to Moriarty who ultimately came to possess his soul.

Porlock had a son who he had raised in Europe after his wife died giving birth. His son was unaware of the true nature of his father's work and Porlock had been diligent about keeping Moriarty from ever reaching into his son's life. That desire for good may have been the goad that moved him to act as an informer and provide me with information vital to my removal of the evil Moriarty from this life.

The tentacles of the Moriarty empire reached throughout Europe. At a moment's notice, he was able to install his agents in various positions, or to establish them in temporary situations in order to achieve any outcome he desired. His operatives were all given faultless aliases, identities and papers. These were never forged, as Moriarty had his own creatures within the government agencies who could issue any official document required. Even Mycroft was at a loss to trace or even explain Moriarty's access to the highest reaches of international government, banking, diplomacy, even the police and military of the major powers.

And so, Porlock had unusual knowledge that had been slowly gained over the many years he served Moriarty. His words in the note to me in 1888, 'I can see that he suspects me,' were chilling for their implication. Yet, Porlock remained in Moriarty's inner circle for three more years. When Moriarty disappeared over the falls, Porlock gained his freedom and he adopted one of Moriarty's stock of identities and returned to London where he evened the score by meeting with Mycroft to whom he gave the particulars that would break what remained of the Moriarty organisation. He then quietly disappeared into the human mass forever.

Porlock was present during that ultimate struggle between evil and good at Meiringen. He played his part to the end as directed by his master, guiding and staging the events leading to the ultimate solution. Fred Porlock was Peter Steiler, the Elder.

25

As this third decade of the Twentieth Century comes to a close, I believe the world is ready to accept the revelations of one of the most disturbing cases in my experience, an acceptance it was not ready to extend in 1887.

The month was July. The place was a squalid half-timbered house in Tripe Alley, Lamb's Conduit, off Park Lane, a fetid, dank quarter housing a population of human denizens that can only be described as vile mammals. All that was wrong with London was quartered in Lamb's Conduit and its warren of crooked arteries, a nether-world that—were it not already there—would necessitate Dickens to conjure it into being.

Extending under the quarter for several blocks in all directions is a great, subterranean cistern built centuries earlier by engineers of the early Roman city of Londinium. Once a marvel of fresh water storage, the cistern now is a rat-infested settling pond for the refuse of thousands living in the tenements extending south to the river.

The half-timbered house in Tripe Alley, sagging and leaning from a hundred years of age and neglect, presented a low, beamed door to the cobbled alleyway, windows shuttered against time, and nothing other than silence and darkness to recommend its brooding interior. It was within this ill-promise of a house where human cruelty reached the heights of the bizarre and grotesque.

London and, indeed, all major cities of Europe and Asia, generated massive demands for certain commodities that could only be supplied by human donors. These included raw organs, fresh bodies, skeletons, limbs, heads, brains, eyes, and even complete sets of teeth and fillets of skin. Nothing of flesh or bone was ever wasted; all found eager takers at good prices on any given day of the year.

For the London medical colleges, there was a particular demand for preserved bodies, body parts and organs. These were used for dissection and study in order to teach anatomy and physiology. Privileged was the future surgeon who obtained his own collection of embalmed organs of the abdominal cavity in order to perfect his art over the course of several years of training, or the nascent oculist who was able to possess sets of preserved eyes of various sizes and conditions upon which to perfect the delicate surgical techniques of his chosen trade. Orthopaedists, apprentices or journeymen, required a constant supply of bones in order to experiment and perfect their mechanical and structural efficacies. The growing specialisation of medicine and surgery in the 1880s by itself added to the swelling need for bodies and diverse parts. All in all, the flesh and bone trade of London was a significant and profitable subterranean trade and one that could not be supplied sufficiently only through the brutish expedients of body-snatching and grave-robbing. Demand outpaced supply and that always creates a lucrative criminal alternative. Ever since the emergence of the sailing ships, the demand for sailors to man the ships has created a criminal trade in fresh seamen. The demand for diamonds, gold, silver and coal doomed countless men to a life of forced labour in the world's pits. The demand for tobacco, rum and sugar created the inhumanity of the slave trade. No matter where one looks in history, the human body—in one state or another—has had value and been the subject of criminal trade. And, in Tripe Alley, that trade reached a new height of efficiency.

For several years, Lestrade and his fellow inspectors at Scotland Yard were aware of a growing catalogue of missing persons from a seemingly random group of classes of society, including gentry to servant classes and all classes between. There was no borough or area of the city where the missing were concentrated, and none where they were spared. The list of missing, which had grown over three years to more than five-hundred as close as could be determined, was random as to male and female, age, occupation, class, education, or any other classification. The only thing in common was that their physical bodies had simply disappeared. Great care had been taken not to inform the public about this out-of-control and unexplained record of missing people.

One fog-laden afternoon in the winter of 1887, Inspectors Lestrade, Morton, Hill, Forbes, Patterson, MacKinnon, and Jones called upon me in Montague Street. In turn, they each spoke of their combined knowledge and experience with numerous missing persons and asked for my assistance in finding what they felt to be an organized malevolent causation for the disappearances. I, of course, readily agreed to look into the matter and, to assure myself a free hand in applying my own methods, indicated my preference for remaining in the background and giving the official police all credit where due.

Suffice it to say that my investigations over the next four months were exhaustive, requiring a great amount of my time. It was necessary to discover the circumstances at the time of the disappearances of nearly four-hundred individuals who were at least partially known to Scotland Yard, and another one-hundred who were not. For many of these unfortunates, the official records contained the information I sought; for many others I had to interview those who last had contact with the missing. All of that data then had to be arranged and synthesized in order to arrive at some nominal working hypothesis. By May of 1887, I had completed my foundation work and was able to look at the indications of this enormous investigative effort.

Two facts emerged: the victims were truly random and had nothing whatsoever in common except that they were alive and human; and most of the victims, when last viewed, had been either walking, riding, or intending to travel in a direction that—when plotted on a map—pointed most often to Hyde Park. From these findings, I made the working hypothesis that the victims were taken by others who were traveling in the same direction; and that direction and—therefore—ultimate destination of nearly five hundred Londoners was Hyde Park or its nearby environs.

A subsequent series of five deductive steps of inference, logic, fact, overlay, and observation extending over a period of thirty-two days, had led me to Lamb's Conduit and Tripe Alley, in the immediate Hyde Park area, as the one potential destination that nearly all of the victims may have had in common. The fifth step in my process—observation—required my concealment, and that of my agents, twenty-four hours a day for a fortnight in a filthy service area at the bifurcation of Tripe Alley from Lamb's Conduit where we observed twelve occurrences of different parties of three inebriants entering the half-timbered house and, shortly after, two of the original three re-emerging from the house, sober, and making their way out of the quarter. The missing inebriant was always the individual in the middle of the staggering group of three when they entered the house, a person who apparently was either drunk or drugged and was supported and propelled by the outer two, the two who always re-appeared and departed the area. I had now made a connection between the random disappearances of hundreds of Londoners from all walks of life and the sinister house in Tripe Alley.

I required additional information that could only be obtained from the wretched cast-offs who lived in the dark existence of Lamb's Conduit. Disguised as a soup and suet-man, I frequented the grime-caked gin hall that served as the quarter's drinking establishment. For over two weeks, after gaining acquaintance by liberal standings to glasses of gin and hot water, and through subtle inquiries of numerous broken men and women, the details of which need not detain us here, I developed a complete understanding of how one could earn four bob by simply conveying an unsuspecting visitor to the house in Tripe Alley for 'a spot of drink and pleasure.' None of my informers knew what took place in the ancient house after they delivered their 'four bob visitors' nor did they know who the inhabitants of the house were except to say they were Lascars or Malays and probably opium sellers.

By promising my informers four bob each and with the surety of an added four bob from the receivers, I contracted them to convey me inside the house late the next evening. I took the precaution to arm myself with a six-cartridge pistol secreted inside one of my boots and instructing Lestrade to have his men ready to secure the house and its occupants at any sign of trouble.

When we had gained Tripe Alley, my convey-ors did not knock at the low door, but pushed it open and motioned me inside, a fast entry that made for a fast disappearance and less chance of being seen. Inside was a vestibule with a second door. Three raps quickly resulted in the opening of a sliding view hole and the ap-pearance of a Lascar's greasy face and menacing black eyes. The door opened and I was inside. My compan-ions were each paid their four bob and hurried away. Immediately, the Lascar encircled my neck with a thick rope, taking me by surprise, while two others suddenly appeared, pinioned my arms, and walked me to a large room with three others, two men and a woman, tied to large iron rings in the overhead beams. In front of us was the most grotesque chimera I had ever witnessed.

Three human beings were inside a narrow glass chamber at the end of the room. Another three were just emerging from the chamber and three more—the three tied to the rings with me—were apparently being readied to be next to enter the narrow glass booth. On three surgical tables were an additional three bodies in process of dissection by three bearded men with long boning knives wearing bloody, leather aprons. The bodies being cut apart drained their fluids through a large grate in the floor leading, doubtless, to the ancient cistern below and its foul human wastes of all descriptions.

The glass chamber, having received its next three victims, was closed and a large, wheel valve opened. It filled the glass chamber with a thick, yellow cloud of gas and the odour was unmistakable, taking me back to my laboratory days at university: Paradol, the taxidermic embalming gas first developed for preservation of animals for museums that permeates the pores and, with a living specimen still breathing, fixes the tissues of the body through saturation oxygen bonding. Only three minutes of living respiration are necessary and the body emerges from the Paradol chamber, fully, permanently, and perfectly preserved *in perpetuity*. Here, in this chamber of horrors, Paradol was being used by the three bearded dissecting taxidermists to preserve living human beings. The horrific house in Tripe Lane was a human abattoir, an Industrial Revolution processing plant for bodies, bones, organs and flesh for the Victorian medical trade.

Noting the mechanical process for the processing of the human victims, I concluded that these vile vivisectionists had, long since, dropped their guard as victim after victim succumbed to their industrial mechanisation. When they untied me from the rings, preparing to move me to the next phase of the process, my hands were momentarily free and, pistol to hand, I struck the nearest Lascar in the temple, felling him unconscious. Each of the other two, I fired at a femur and shattered their legs rendering them helpless. The three dissectionists laid down their knives and surrendered themselves to the remaining four cartridges in my pistol pointed at them.

The sound of the gunshots brought Lestrade and his men who stormed the house, taking the Lascars, the taxidermists and two others, found in a below stairs warehouse of bodies and body part specimens, into custody.

The Home Secretary, unable to reconcile the horrors of the Paradol Chamber and the Tripe Alley charnel house of unspeakable atrocities with the sensibilities of the British public, placed the records of the entire matter in the Most Secret vault. The butchers led Scotland Yard to the men at the top of the inhuman ring of flesh sellers and, as one might expect, found several of the wayward scions of two of the most respected families in England. In the end, all of the participants in the Horror of the Paradol Chamber were executed in anonymity and their body parts taken to the anatomical dissection laboratories of each of the medical universities to disappear forever from the list of British humanity.

26

There is a bench at the north side of Russell Square, facing south, where the sun warms one in the morning, penetrating the broad leaves of the ancient plane trees shading the park. A coffee seller, close by in a small building bordering the pathway, offers the finest coffee of my experience: hot, strong, rich and velvet with Devon cream. This is one of my favourite places in the whole of London.

From my seat on the bench, I observe the world through the years. I have been perfecting my powers of observation for so long that every person strolling through the park is known fully to me with a glance. Since Mycroft's passing from life, I have had to be content with observational contests with myself. Mycroft was always the better of the two of us; his powers were far greater than mine, but he seldom employed them. He would look from my window in Montague Street and describe each person walking past as to age, occupation, physical health, marriage state, degree of wealth or poverty, and even an accurate appraisal of their sins and vices. Mycroft possessed what can only be described as 'the mind's eye.'

We once were engaged in our game of observation while having coffee in the Officers' Room of the Foreign Office where we observed a man sitting reading a newspaper. Only his lower body and his fingers extended from the pages of the newspaper, all else being hidden behind. My attention focused on his trouser cuffs and his shoes. I asked Mycroft, 'What do you make of him?' and he immediately replied, 'Visiting classical guitarist from Spain.' I had already deduced Spain from the cut of the last of his shoes, but Mycroft had added 'visiting' from the Spanish newspaper he was reading and 'classical guitarist' from the slanted filing of the elongated fingernails of the first three fingers of his right hand.

I had a great regard for my brother. Our brains bound us together in a way that was different from our other siblings. We seldom saw each other, yet we sensed each other constantly, as if we drew on each other's brain power for interpretation or monitoring. I believe Mycroft was aware at moments when I was faced with danger, and I knew—or more accurately, felt—whenever he was charged with great responsibility for the security of Britain. Together, we were far more effective than we were individually. Had we both gone into government service, we would have been able to alter, at will, the history of Great Britain or Europe; had we both gone into the detection of crime, we would have been more successful than Scotland Yard or any other police force; and if we had both gone into crime itself, we would have dominated the underworld.

Our latent potential, however, was held in check by our essential laziness. Mycroft could barely be induced to stir outside his rooms, his offices or his club and if the problem did not involve the government, it did not involve Mycroft's mind. I picked and chose only the problems that interested me. We were both pre-eminent in what we did, and we both did do great work, but we did only that which was within our spheres of interest.

Mycroft had his own commonplace books which, in his precise and spare writing, recorded over two-hundred governmental crises in which he was instrumental averting or solving over his long, if sedentary, public service career, ending just a year before his death. These cases chronicle modern British history; indeed, Mycroft *is* modern British history.

Of course, his casebooks can never be revealed to the public; I am the only person who has ever read what Mycroft wrote in the long hours spanning the long years alone in his rooms. Each of the two-hundred-seventeen critical interventions that rested upon the integrity and intelligence of Mycroft equally shaped Britain's place in the world as we know it between 1865 and 1925 and, indeed, beyond. Mycroft made and broke Prime Ministers, cabinet members, admirals and generals, ministers, diplomats, high justices, and even royals; but, he served his queen and kings with the steadfast and unblemished fealty of a First Knight. Mycroft was the link between the monarchs and the people of Britain; he possessed a mind of such purity that only he could eliminate the domestic and foreign political influences and steer destiny to the ultimate truth and good for Britain. And, no one knows who he truly was, few even his name. His great legacy to the country is the fact that he appears to have never existed, a form of selflessness that only a very few are ever able to achieve.

I have devised and constructed an elaborate and labyrinthine perpetual storage and archiving of Mycroft's chronicles that will assure that they never appear until the year 2027, one hundred years after his death and long after the historic events he shaped. In that year, they will emerge from the past and be assigned to the Library of the British Museum where Mycroft will, at long last, receive proper recognition for his service to crown and country.

※

27

Mycroft's commonplace books call to mind the disposition of my own nearly three yards of half-inch thick notebooks containing my written case notations from the whole of my career which has extended to this day upon which I write this chapter, as I am presently engaged on a most interesting little problem for a great lady of Teck involving a smoked salmon and the five furlong marker at Epsom Downs.

My detailed written notes contained in the two-hundred and six commonplace notebooks are in addition to those of Watson's and it is my intention to soon combine them and place them with the Keeper of the Archives at Exeter College Library with instructions as to future access to their contents. It is also my intent to endow the college with the means to professionally index both my case notes and Watson's and to establish an historical criminology research collection at Exeter College.

The public will little remember my career, but I believe the professional detectives of Britain and Europe may find my case notes instructive and, through their study, may improve the art and science of observation, deduction and factual reasoning within their investigative forces. A new era is approaching in crime detection when forensic evidence will move to the fore and science will play an increasingly important role in bringing about proper justice. Fingerprinting will become much more significant in assembling evidence against criminals. Fingerprints offer evidence that every human has completely unique patterns on the skin of the fingers. In the same manner, I believe every human being has a unique signature in their cellular structure and one day this will be used as irrefutable evidence when skin, hair or body fluids are found, analysed and linked to the criminal who committed the crime.

It will be impossible to find men with brains the equal of mine, but it will be possible to train good men to use my methods and to augment them with the advances in forensic sciences and, in so doing, to stem the tide of criminal activity and improve the accuracy of conclusive detection and prosecution.

I have thought often of the great benefit that could be had through the establishment of a university dedicated solely to the study of criminology. We have such universities for the preparation of the military. We have great universities of medicine. We have dedicated studies in the law. But our forces fighting the criminals are schooled in the streets, taught only to apply brute force and repetitive routine, and given little reward for innovation or intellect. If every detective were to have the kind of training that we require for a doctor, engineer, lawyer, or army major, the quality of police work would improve greatly and benefit the British people immeasurably.

My experience is that university trained men are better police inspectors. They possess, to a greater degree, the ability to think which, in turn, gives them a greater capacity to reason and form more accurate conclusions. And, more often, they are able to separate their ego from their investigative processes. The most detrimental characteristics of the bog-standard Scotland Yard inspector brought up through the ranks are stubbornness and arrogance. The best of them may only get forty percent of the essential elements of their cases correct and accurate. I have endeavoured to assist wherever I have been asked to offer my insights, and it has made a difference, but there is much to be improved upon.

Until such time in future as the casebooks are opened to study, those who care to do their Upper First in the art and science of detection will soon have my *magnum opus* for instruction: *The Science of Deduction and Detection.* I have made discrete mention of it to the Prime Minister with the quiet intimation that it may be best employed as required study by all Inspector level detectives or even all those new to the detective grade within Scotland Yard. He has indicated encouragement for its imminent adoption.

28

There is one aspect of my life I should like to set down here. It has never been mentioned and would not be mentioned except for my appreciation for an individual's loyalty and friendship towards me expressed from time to time by that steadfast individual.

My life has not encouraged what others call friends. I have been far too occupied with my work to devote the time required by relationships with friends. Watson is as close as I have come to a friend; even he, however, has always been more of a colleague. I perceive that friends reach into the private portions of one's life, whereas colleagues are content to remain within the latitudes of the work and the shared interests.

Friends can demand time from one when time is not available, and that can create tensions that distract one from the concentration on the problem at hand. Imprecise reasoning in one's profession can never be excused by the outside demands of mental effort and time by friends. One chooses: intellectual excellence or emotion-based relationships. My path was ever clear and direct.

A time comes, however, in one's life when momentary diversion, such as that a friend may offer, can be of some benefit. Even the precision machine benefits from a drop or two of oil to reduce wear from friction. An hour of quiet reflection and sharing of the simple shadings of the day can be refreshing and, like the drop of oil, reduce tension and offer respite from intense concentration. Even a light meal, taken together, can be a pleasant interlude in an otherwise pressing schedule of work and mental stimulation.

In 1922, nearly seven years ago come August, I made the acquaintance of one whom I have come to call my friend. An older gentleman, he called upon me one day unannounced and returned several times before I was able to gather the threads of his mystery. It took several visits and my personal assurances before Mrs Hunter would answer his request to call upon me without a look of foreboding and displeasure, but that was the nature of my independent caller. He was a bit unkempt and had a slight limp; his eyes were what is called rheumy, as if illness or overindulgence were behind their watery appearance. After taking a chair, he would—from time to time—drop off into a light sleep, seemingly tired from exertions that were unknown. My observation of his scarred ears and oversized thumbs told me that he had battled others in his hard life, perhaps at sea or among those who prowled the docks. At first, he had a somewhat objectionable odour from a lack of bathing. Later, with some small encouragement from Ms Hunter, his toilet was measurably improved and his general health gained vigour.

At first, our discussions were perfunctory, relegated to my questions and his few grunts. As we progressed, a clarity of expression developed and we had great long and wide-ranging discussions that delved into each of our inner interests.

My friend has spent seven years now visiting me for a portion of each day in Montague Street, generally for a late breakfast. He delights in Mrs Hunter's fried eggs and streaky bacon. I have never called upon him at his home and, indeed, have no idea where it is to be found. I am told he has been seen strolling evenings in Montague Place, just a block or two away.

He asks little of me but offers a reserved enjoyment and companionship to one who is now seventy-seven years old. His name is Albert. While of mixed descent, one would describe him as a yellow tabby with three white feet.

29

My medical needs were provided for a number of years by Dr Moore Agar. Since his retirement in 1919, I have been attended by his son, Dr Morris Agar who took over his father's Harley Street practice. Young Dr Agar has made a name for himself through his skill as a diagnostician. Where others are unable to reach a diagnosis in difficult cases, Dr Agar is requested as a consultant to establish the accurate and definitive diagnosis. He uses methods that are quite like my own in solving difficult problems: knowledge, observation and reasoning coupled with testing to reach one or more hypotheses which can be refined by careful questioning and investigation of the physical evidence.

While the state of my health was previously not a matter in which I took the slightest interest, there were several periods of physical exhaustion brought about by prolonged work that required complete rests to restore my usually strong constitution. In 1920, I spent a week aboard a Japanese freighter docked in the East End of London working as a cook while preparing my net for the captain, the poisoner Shigawa, who had used the venom of the Fugu Pufferfish to kill three Formosan emissaries to Great Britain negotiating support for a revolution against China. He introduced the venom into their soup during a dinner hosted by the Foreign Office. They died within four minutes. The Prime Minister requested that I bring the murderer into custody and assist in resolving the unfortunate embarrassment to the government.

During the miasmic week aboard the freighter, I contracted an unusual Asian malady from infected onions that struck me down within a five-day period of incubation. Dr Agar manipulated the symptoms and clues and isolated the insidious *Matsumato speagorea retarges*, a microscopic worm that invades the tissues of the heart after entering the body through the tear ducts and, in a week of astounding replication and growth, spreads millions of worms throughout the body via the bloodstream, blocking the capillary system, severely restricting the flow of oxygenated blood, and ultimately causing death from asphyxiation in ninety-five percent of the victims. The only possible treatment is the injection of the purified blood of the Carcassian centipede which contains high concentrations of caustic Steraemaniasis, a potent fulminator and the only known toxin to kill the *Matsumato* worm.

Dr Agar appealed to the Royal College of Physicians in Edinburgh and a sufficient quantity of the rare injectable Steraemaniasis was obtained from the only research laboratory in Great Britain with a supply in time to preserve my life. I was back to work in two months, albeit weakened from the disease and the treatment. Dr Agar has stated that the parasite can tunnel deep into the heart tissue and lie encapsulated and dormant for up to twelve years and, in a quarter of the victims, a second acute phase is experienced and is, invariably, fatal within days as further injections are ineffective.

Prior to the initial attack, however, I was able to complete my case and see the murderous Japanese freighter captain in the hands of Scotland Yard. He was remanded for trial, found guilty, was condemned and hanged the next day at Wormwood Scrubs and the affair quietly filed in the records of the Foreign Office which declined to become involved in the delicate and now Most Secret Formosa matter.

[Editor's Note: At this point the manuscript of *Montague Notations* ends. Two small quarter-sheets of light blue paper in the same handwriting were found inserted between the final two leaves. One had the notation, "Dr Agar, half-two, 5 July inst." The other, also in the same handwriting, contained a brief outline for four additional chapters, numbered 30 through 33. All attempts to locate Dr Agar's appointment book containing his schedule for 5 July 1929 or his patient medical records have met with failure.]